'You're not sending me away, are you

Gaby went on desperately, 'Because if you'll give me another chance I promise I will stop myself from being so noticeable.'

'And how will you accomplish that?' Ethan asked drily.

'I'll only speak when I'm spoken to, wear thick woollen stockings, a bra with no uplift,' she said, half laughing, half serious, 'and I'll never criticise your decorating again.'

Abigail Gordon began writing some years ago at the suggestion of her sister, who is herself an established writer. She has found it an absorbing and fulfilling way of expressing herself, and feels that in the medical romance there is an opportunity to present realistically strong dramatic situations with which readers can identify. Abigail lives in a Cheshire village near Stockport, and is widowed with three grown-up sons and several grandchildren.

Recent titles by the same author:

CRISIS FOR CASSANDRA

RESPONDING TO TREATMENT

BY
ABIGAIL GORDON

DID YOU PURCHASE THIS BOOK WITHOUT A COVER?
If you did, you should be aware it is **stolen property** as it was reported *unsold and destroyed* by a retailer. Neither the Author nor the publisher has received any payment for this book.

All the characters in this book have no existence outside the imagination of the author, and have no relation whatsoever to anyone bearing the same name or names. They are not even distantly inspired by any individual known or unknown to the author, and all the incidents are pure invention.

All rights reserved including the right of reproduction in whole or in part in any form. This edition is published by arrangement with Harlequin Enterprises II B.V. The text of this publication or any part thereof may not be reproduced or transmitted in any form or by any means, electronic or mechanical, including photocopying, recording, storage in an information retrieval system, or otherwise, without the written permission of the publisher.

This book is sold subject to the condition that it shall not, by way of trade or otherwise, be lent, resold, hired out or otherwise circulated without the prior consent of the publisher in any form of binding or cover other than that in which it is published and without a similar condition including this condition being imposed on the subsequent purchaser.

*MILLS & BOON, the Rose Device and
LOVE ON CALL are trademarks of the publisher.
Harlequin Mills & Boon Limited,
Eton House, 18-24 Paradise Road, Richmond, Surrey TW9 1SR*

© Abigail Gordon 1996

ISBN 0 263 79996 4

*Set in Times 10 on $11^{1}/_{2}$ pt. by
Rowland Phototypesetting Limited
Bury St Edmunds, Suffolk*

03-9612-48955

Made and printed in Great Britain

CHAPTER ONE

THERE was a wedding taking place at the small stone church opposite as Gaby wheeled her bulging case out of the village railway station. She paused, her intention to hail the first taxi she saw becoming sidetracked as a radiant blonde bride on the arm of a striking dark-haired man appeared out of the gloom of the church and stood framed in its arched doorway.

A true romantic, Gaby never could resist a wedding and the need to find transport to take her to her journey's end was momentarily forgotten as she crossed over the road to where beribboned wedding cars stood at the church gates.

There was a crowd watching the proceedings from the churchyard and she joined them, noting that those representing the bride and groom consisted of just a chubby middle-aged bridesmaid in a smart pink suit, a ruddy-complexioned man of a similar age and a dark-haired boy.

Engrossed in the scene, Gaby wasn't aware that she was the subject of some curiosity. Heads were turning to observe the olive-skinned girl with the high cheekbones and dark glossy hair that hung in tendrils around her face. Here was an attractive stranger. . .and a travelling one at that, if the huge suitcase was anything to go by.

A photographer was fussing over the bridal couple and as he did so Gaby looked around her. The people in the churchyard were for the most part casually dressed, obviously made up from village people and passers-by, whilst the wedding guests were clustered around the church porch.

Two nurses clutching cartons of confetti were standing not far away, poised at the ready, and she wondered in which branch of the area's health authority they were employed. She would find out soon enough, she reckoned, and in the meantime she supposed she ought to be on her way.

There was a man standing just to the side of her who didn't seem to qualify as a casual onlooker. In a smart grey suit, with a flower in his buttonhole, he looked like a guest. Yet he was standing aloof from the wedding party, his face, beneath hair as golden as that of the bride, set in a sombre mould and his blue eyes shadowed.

Gaby's fertile imagination began to work. Maybe he was a jilted suitor, wishing that he'd spoken up when the vicar had asked if anyone knew of any just cause why the wedding shouldn't proceed, or perhaps he wasn't a guest at all and the buttonhole was just a gesture.

Telling herself that she was crazy idling away the time here in the churchyard when she'd been travelling most of the day and still hadn't reached her destination, she grabbed the handle of her case and turned swiftly, only to discover that the man she'd been speculating about had also decided to depart and as they collided he almost knocked her off her feet.

His hand flew out immediately to steady her and as his eyes widened in surprise Gaby was piqued to discover that *she* hadn't impinged on *his* consciousness. He'd been too engrossed in the wedding to notice her standing nearby, although it now looked as if he was on the move. 'I'm sorry,' he said stiffly, removing his grip once he saw that she's regained her balance. 'My fault entirely.'

'Yes, it was,' she said serenely. 'You weren't looking where you were going and took me by surprise.'

It was true, he had, in more ways than one. For instance, there weren't many men who didn't notice her. She was used to being admired, chatted up, invited out, but, though it was gratifying, she invariably refused because she was Georgio's girl.

At least she'd thought she was, until she'd arrived in Italy to nurse her grandmother through her last long illness. It was then that she'd discovered that Georgio Rossi, who she'd dated constantly when they'd both been training in London, had developed other ideas once he'd got back to Sorrento and slotted himself into his father's hotel chain.

The man in the grey suit was observing her case. 'Can I direct you anywhere?' he offered. 'You appear to be a stranger in the village.'

Gaby gave him the wide friendly smile that had melted far more restrained men than this.

'Yes. I need to be pointed in the direction of Cleeve House.'

'Cleeve House?' he echoed with surprise in his blue eyes again. 'Sally Barnes's place?'

'I do believe that is the name of my landlady-to-be,' she told him breezily as she reached for the handle of her case again.

'Ah, of course, you'll be a new lodger?' he said with the restrained politeness of someone who is wishing that they hadn't got involved.

'You've guessed it,' she told him, 'and I won't be sorry to get there. I feel as if I've been travelling for ever.'

He managed a mild show of interest. 'Where have you come from?'

'Italy.'

He was observing the long black velvet skirt and low-cut white blouse that she'd chosen to travel in, and as he raised his eyes to her tanned face and the glossy hair framing it there was a bruised sort of wariness in them. But why for heaven's sake? She didn't usually have *that* effect on men but the fair-haired stranger was asking the obvious question as he took in her dark beauty.

'You're Italian?'

'Part of me is and the rest is pure Brum,' she told him laughingly.

He tried again and this time she had his full attention. 'You're from Birmingham?'

'Mmm. My mother was Italian and my father a Midlands man.' Her glance flicked to the bride and groom now starting to move towards them along the wide path of the churchyard. 'On the face of it not perhaps as suitable a match as this wedding couple appear to be—' her voice had softened '—but it seemed to work.'

Gaby averted her face. She must be going weak in the head, telling a complete stranger about her origins. If this was how weddings were going to affect her she'd better stay clear of them in future.

Maybe it was because she'd seen herself in this sort of circumstance on Giorgio's arm and had had her hopes dashed, and with the thought of the young Italian's hot dark eyes and sensual lips the golden-haired man at her side seemed even more cool and remote.

She made to pick up her case, suddenly anxious to go before the bridal couple got level, but her new acquaintance took it out of her hand and said levelly, 'Let *me* carry this for you. It looks as if you've brought everything but the kitchen sink.'

'I suppose I have,' she agreed wryly. 'It contains all my worldly goods.'

He was only half listening. His eyes were on the fair-skinned bride now only feet away and, as Gaby watched, his lips tightened, but as the bridal couple moved on towards their wedding car his attention reverted back to her.

'Cleeve House is a couple of hundred yards along the road,' he said flatly. 'We can either walk there or I'll put the case in my car and drive you.'

'I'd like to walk,' she said immediately. 'It will give me the chance to see some of my new surroundings. Er, that is if you don't mind carrying the case.'

'No, of course not. It's only a short walk,' and he led the way, taking her out of the churchyard by a side gate that was nowhere near the wedding party.

As he walked beside her without speaking Gaby said easily, 'I feel I should introduce myself.'

He turned his head and eyed her without curiosity. 'Yes?'

'My name is Gabriella Dennison, but most people call me Gaby. What's yours?'

'Ethan Lassiter,' he said briefly after a moment's silence.

He halted outside a double-fronted stone house just as the wedding car went past, its occupants oblivious to everyone but themselves. Walking up the flagged path, he said formally, 'This is Cleeve House and, now, if you will excuse me I have to get back to the wedding.'

Her eyes widened. 'You're a guest?'

'Yes. Why? Does that surprise you?'

Her eyes flicked over the smart grey suit, the flower in his buttonhole, and she told him, 'Not in one way because you look the part, but you didn't seem to be with the rest of them. It was as if you were aloof from it all and I would never have butted into your afternoon like I have if I'd known. Your friends must have wondered where on earth you were going when they saw you leave the churchyard carrying my case.'

His face had closed up. 'Don't worry about that. It will probably be the most useful thing I do today,' and with a brief nod he strode off in the direction of the church.

As she watched him go Gaby was aware that the interest had been all on her part in their brief encounter. The man called Ethan Lassiter had treated her with a restrained sort of courtesy but his mind had been elsewhere, and if he had been her type she might have felt peeved that she'd made so little impression on him.

When she rang the bell the door was opened by a tall copper-haired woman in beige trousers and an emerald green sweater, and when she saw Gaby standing on the step she said smilingly, 'Let me guess... you are Gabriella Dennison.'

Gaby smiled back. 'Right first time...and you're Sally Barnes?'

'None other,' she replied, 'and that being so let me help you with your case.

'What sort of a journey did you have?' she asked as they climbed a curved staircase to a sunlit bedroom at the back of the house.

'Not bad,' Gaby told her. 'As I mentioned when we spoke on the phone I've come from Sorrento. Naples airport was busy but once the flight was under way I managed a couple of hours sleep, which has been something in short supply while I've been nursing my *nonna*.'

She was observing her landlady while she spoke and Sally asked whimsically, 'What's wrong? Am I not what you expected?'

'No, you're not,' Gaby told her frankly. 'I always think of landladies as wearing grey cardigans and having their hair in a bun but you don't look much older than me.'

'Which exempts me from the cardigan and the bun?' she questioned laughingly and then, on a more businesslike note, 'We eat at seven—judge me when you've had your first meal at Cleeve House, eh?'

'There was a wedding at the church near the railway station,' Gaby said quickly as Sally Barnes made to go back downstairs. 'I stopped to watch it for a few minutes.'

The other woman smiled. 'That would be Cassandra Bryant and Bevan Marsland. She is sister manager at Springfield Community Hospital and he is our new GP. You'll be seeing quite a bit of them both if you're going to be employed at Springfield.'

Ah, Gaby thought, so that's who they are. It was on the tip of her tongue to ask Sally Barnes if she knew the reticent wedding guest, Ethan Lassiter, but she didn't. If he lived in the village she was bound to meet him again and it would be interesting to see if he was any more relaxed on further acquaintance.

As she began to unpack Gaby put the meeting in the churchyard to the back of her mind and let the memories of six traumatic months in Italy take over her thoughts.

Although there had been no definite commitment between them, Gaby had taken it for granted that Giorgio cared for her but she'd been put straight about that supposition when she'd discovered that the moment he'd got back home he had taken himself a wife.

To arrive at her *nonna's* rented apartment and find her even more sick than she'd been led to believe had been distressing enough, and then discovering that Giorgio had married without having the decency to let her know had almost wiped out her natural bounce—but not quite.

She was a carefree, generous girl, who had no sooner finished her nurse's training than the opportunity to put what she'd learned into practice had come from an unexpected source—not on the wards of some big hospital but in Sorrento, her mother's birthplace.

During the six months she'd nursed her grandmother there had been little time to fret over Giorgio's change of heart, if it could be described as that, as on the few occasions when their paths had crossed he'd been eager to make it clear that he would be prepared to continue their relationship behind his wife's back.

'I married Gina for the sake of the business,' he'd wheedled. 'Her father promised to put money into the hotel chain if we got married and my parents were all for it.'

Gaby had eyed him with angry scorn. 'I'll bet! You're sure it wasn't a means to an end? To make sure that his forthcoming grandchild had its father's name?' She had tossed her ebony mane. 'Whatever the reason you married Gina she was obviously a better catch than a wet-behind-the-ears nurse without a lira to her name!'

As he had stepped towards her pleadingly she'd thumped him in the chest and told him angrily, 'Get lost, Giorgio! I'm not mistress material!' And then she had returned to the sick-room, to the company of someone who really *did* love her.

After her *nonna's* death she'd spent some time sorting out her affairs and clearing the apartment and while she'd been doing it she'd got in touch with the NHS in the Midlands to see what vacancies were on offer.

The post of staff nurse in a big Birmingham hospital that she'd been offered at the end of her training had of course been filled. The authorities weren't going to hold it for six months, and as there were staff cuts in progress all over the health service there wasn't much on offer.

When the chance of a similar position at a cottage-type hospital at the foot of the Cotswolds had been passed on to her she hadn't hesitated in accepting, even though it was hardly going to be the action-packed entry into health care that she'd envisaged for herself.

The personnel people from the health authority that she'd been communicating with had recommended Sally Barnes's guest house if she was going to need accommodation, and Gaby had phoned Sally from Italy to make the necessary arrangements.

And now, late on a Saturday afternoon, she was here, raring to get her teeth into the job at Springfield Community Hospital but with a few doubts inside her as to how tasty a bite it was going to be.

When Gaby went downstairs Sally, in a tall chef's hat and a striped apron, came out of the kitchen to introduce her to the other three boarders at present staying there.

There was an elderly American, touring Britain, who was on a short stay. Then there was Charles Basset, a young male teacher, who had recently been drafted into the village school and was waiting for his house purchase to go through and lastly but, to Gaby's bright gaze, by no means the least, a big, bearded man with merry brown eyes, who was introduced to her as Noah Chaplin, a construction engineer.

'I hope you won't feel too outnumbered by all these men,' Sally said when the introductions were over. 'And I might as well warn you that there's still one more to come.'

As a key turned in the lock she said, 'And here he is, my husband Robert, the brains of the outfit. He does the thinking and I do the work,' and to take the sting out of the comment she kissed the most recent arrival with unconcealed enthusiasm.

The food was delicious, the company pleasant enough, and not the least abashed by the fact that she was the only female present Gaby did the meal justice.

'We're all going to the pub,' the burly builder told her when they'd finished. He nodded towards the American. 'Hank here can't get his fill of rural England. You're welcome to come along if you want.'

Gaby hesitated. She was tired but on the other hand she couldn't remember when last she'd had a night out. 'Yes. I'd like that,' she said, 'but it won't be for long. I need to catch up on my beauty sleep.'

He guffawed. 'What! A bonny young thing like you? I've got a daughter similar age to you an' she don't know what sleep is. Her ma and me never hear her come in at night.'

Gaby joined in his laughter. 'Yes, but I'll bet she hasn't been nursing someone terminally ill for the last few months, has she?'

His face sobered. 'That what you've been doin', girlie? Well, in that case, I'd say you need fun just as much as sleep, though what fun you'll get out o' me, old Hank and that po-faced schoolteacher I don't know, but Sally and Robert'll be coming to liven us up when they've done the washing-up, I dare say.'

'How long are you staying in the village?' she asked.

'Until the extension to the motorway e'or yonder is done. If I have to be away from home that's the way it is, but I do like to stay somewhere comfortable while I'm doin' it an' Cleeve House fits the bill nicely. How about you?'

'I'm a nurse and am due to start at Springfield Community Hospital on Monday so I could be staying with Sally and her husband for quite some time—until I can afford a place of my own, I suppose.'

The Goose Inn was small and cosy and, as Gaby settled herself at a table with her three male companions, she was glad she'd come. She'd had a lot of her own company in recent weeks and was now ready to start expanding the horizons that had been so limited during her *nonna's* illness.

She was laughing at something the burly builder had said, her head thrown back and her mouth with its full lips and even white teeth wide with mirth, when the door opened and her acquaintance of the afternoon came strolling in, still in his wedding-guest attire.

To her annoyance she felt the colour rush to her face and knew there was no reason why it should, unless it was because of his expression when he saw her ensconsed as part of the uneven foursome. She could guess what he must be thinking—that she'd soon made herself at home amongst the male population of the village and of course it was true, she had, in a perfectly innocent way.

Getting slowly to her feet, Gaby strolled across to where he had deposited himself beside the bar. She was consumed with an urge to justify herself, though she wasn't sure why. Perhaps it was because he was the first person she'd met after getting off the train, or maybe it was because he hadn't responded to her friendliness like most folk did and she was curious to know what was beneath his reticence.

'Hello, there,' she said as he looked up at the sound of her footsteps behind him. 'How did it go?'

He was eyeing her with guarded eyes again, as if she were some sort of threatening species he'd come across, and instead of deflating her as it had at their earlier meeting now it seemed like a challenge.

'The wedding went very well,' he said casually, 'if that is what you're referring to. The newly-weds have left for the airport on their way to a secret destination, and the rest of us have dispersed after an excellent reception.'

He turned to survey the three men at the table behind them, chatting amicably amongst themselves. 'It would appear that you've settled in satisfactorily.'

'Yes, they're my fellow boarders at Cleeve House,' she told him breezily, aware that his tone was verging on censure. 'They took pity on me and invited me along, otherwise I would have been in my room twiddling my thumbs.' She laughed, devilment in her eyes. 'And I can't say that I've ever had a leaning towards thumb-twiddling.'

He gave a dry smile. 'Is that so? Well, in that case I hope that when next we meet you will be offering me further confirmation of that fact.'

Gaby's brow was creased in puzzlement. What was that supposed to mean? He was expecting them to meet again? Was it a threat or a promise, and what made him so sure they would? But, of course, this was a village and if he lived here then they were bound to meet at some time or other.

The prospect hardly had him hopping with excitement, though, and Gaby was beginning to feel that, having forced her company on him again, he'd had enough of it. It was possible. There was something in the tone of his voice that told her he didn't trust her for some reason.

Perhaps her first guess when she'd seen him in the churchyard had been right. Maybe he *had* been thwarted in love, and if it wasn't the blonde bride maybe there was another woman somewhere who was the cause of his observing her, Gaby, with such a jaundiced eye.

She had met men who'd had a bad experience with one of her own sex and they took it out on every woman they met. Was Ethan Lassiter like that? Surely she didn't remind him of somebody else! He looked like a man who would be drawn more to mature wine than bubbly.

However wild her surmises might be one thing was clear: *she* might be curious about him but *he* wasn't bursting to know anything about her—such as what she was doing in the village, for instance—and if he wasn't going to ask she was damned if she was going to tell him.

'Can I get you a drink?' he asked distantly.

If the offer had been more cordial she would have accepted, if only to prove to herself that she could get through to this offhanded stranger, but she'd already ordered a glass of fresh orange, which by now would have been brought to the table, and in view of the atmosphere prevailing the obvious thing to do was return to the company of her fellow boarders.

However, with an imp of mischief inside her, she couldn't resist the chance to depart with all flags flying and so she told him sweetly, 'No, thanks just the same.

I've ordered a bottle of stout and a packet of pork scratchings.' And with an exaggerated swaying of her slim hips she went back to join the others.

By the time Gaby had seated herself the man from the churchyard was at the door and, as it swung to behind him, she was already regretting her behaviour. He must think her an absolute pest, pushing herself where she wasn't wanted and inventing drinking habits absolutely foreign to her. What was the matter with her? Was she going crazy? Allowing her return to her native England after such a long absence make her behave like an idiot?

The fact that she'd made a fool of herself in front of the first presentable man she'd met since being ditched by Giorgio was like the behaviour of somebody on the rebound, but she hadn't been attracted to Giorgio to *that* extent and in any case, apart from anything else, Ethan Lassiter was fair skinned and the most self-contained man she'd ever met. He was nothing like the olive-skinned, volatile men of the country from which she'd inherited half of her blood. *She'd* always been more attracted to fire than ice so why, for goodness' sake, was she getting herself in such a tizzy over this stranger?

Later that night as she lay in the pleasant bedroom Gaby's mind wouldn't switch off. Outside the open window was the silence of the countryside and it seemed strange, as in London the throb of traffic went on all through the night and in Sorrento there was always noise and bustle as the night life of the famous resort took over. But here in this small Cotswold village there was peace, and she was thankful for it as her mind shuttled to and fro between the strange new present and the sometimes sad and insecure past.

Her vivacious Italian mother had died when Gaby was ten years old, and her father had married again within the year. Jessica, her new stepmother, was a solid, unimaginative woman, contrasting sharply with Bryan Dennison's first wife, but she'd been kind and reasonably supportive to Gaby and the young girl had been happy enough with them.

However, the moment she was old enough she had left home and gone to London to train as a nurse and it was there that she'd met Giorgio, who'd been taking a course in hotel management because his family owned a group of hotels on the Neapolitan peninsula.

The two of them, both young and very attractive and with connections in Sorrento, had been drawn to each other as soon as they'd met and the discovery that the Italian youth had been merely using her to fill up his time in London had been a bitter pill to swallow. But swallow it she had and once it had gone down she'd got on with her life, which for six months had been of a quality that would have daunted many people.

Her Italian grandmother was the person who Gaby had always been closest to after the death of her mother. All her school holidays had been spent with her *nonna* in the colourful town of Sorrento on the Bay of Naples, an arrangement that suited her father and Jessica as they'd invested in a dry-cleaning business and didn't want a restless teenager under their feet.

Just as Gaby had finished her training and was about to start nursing, a neighbour of her *nonna* had rung to say that the old lady was very ill and, as her father had felt that the responsibility wasn't his and Jessica seemed to be in agreement, it was a distraught Gaby who had boarded the first plane out to dash to her *nonna's* bedside.

The old lady had suffered a stroke, which thankfully hadn't taken her speech but had left her badly paralysed and bronchial, and Gaby had been heartbroken to realise that she wasn't going to get better.

Her father and Jessica hadn't attended the funeral and it had been left to her and her *nonna's* few friends to follow the coffin to the cemetery. Gaby had thought sombrely that the months she'd spent in Sorrento had been a time of endings—her grandmother's life, her relationship with Giorgio—and she was desperate for a new beginning, a fresh start, and now it was here.

Today was the first day of the rest of her life. She had come to live and work in new surroundings. She'd already met new people, made new friends, and it was all very strange and exciting.

There was Sally and her husband, Noah, and the other two boarders, and the man she'd already met twice in the few hours she'd been in the village. If anyone should ask her what she remembered most about her first day in this place, it would be a pair of guarded eyes beneath a golden pelt of hair, a firm mouth that indicated strength, determination and something else...implacability, maybe...and it was the memory of that same mouth that was still in her mind as at last sleep took over.

On Monday morning the long velvet skirt and revealing white blouse were discarded for a short-sleeved blue dress that fitted the measurements Gaby had forwarded on to the hospital from Italy. It had been delivered to Cleeve House previously and had been hanging in her wardrobe when she'd arrived.

There was excitement in her this morning. It might

not be St Bartholomew's where she was to make her debut but she couldn't have been more determined to succeed if it had been.

Her long, tangled mane had been brushed into glossy submission and now hung in a thick tail on her shoulders. The make-up she'd used on her striking young face was light and flattering, and on her feet were black low-heeled shoes that were a far cry from the strappy gold sandals she'd arrived in.

She'd gone for a solitary walk the previous day, to familiarise herself with the route to the hospital and its layout, and as she'd stood on a grassy hillock and surveyed the low red brick building with its trim gardens, through which ran a leisurely stream, Gaby had been conscious of a sense of tranquillity. It was a sensation that she'd only ever felt previously in her *nonna*'s company and now, *that* being gone for ever, it would be a bonus were she to find it here.

However, after presenting herself outside the hospital manager's office at Springfield, promptly at eight o'clock, she was to find tranquillity in short supply.

When she went in after a brusque invitation Gaby saw that an elderly, auburn-haired nurse was lying in the centre of the grey pile carpet, clutching at her chest and groaning with pain, and bending over her was Gaby's acquaintance of the churchyard.

As she stared at him in amazement he hissed, 'Don't stand there gaping! Help me to get her onto the couch.'

She ran forward and between them they laid the woman on a leather chesterfield in the corner, and as soon as they'd done so Ethan Lassiter picked up the phone and said with clipped urgency, 'If there's a GP anywhere in the place, send him to my office immediately. Sister Travis has collapsed.'

While he'd been speaking Gaby had been loosening the prostrate woman's clothing and feeling for her pulse. She was deathly pale and her lips had a bluish tinge, and when he hurried back to her side he echoed the thoughts of his newest member of staff.

'Heart, by the looks of it,' he said, glancing urgently at the door. 'Flora had come to my office to discuss hospital matters and she'd no sooner arrived than she developed severe chest pains.'

Gaby could hear swift footsteps on the corridor outside and a second later the door was flung open. When she lifted her head a man in a white coat with limp fair hair and horn-rimmed glasses was observing her, and as he moved quickly towards the semi-conscious woman Ethan Lassiter said in a low voice, 'If I hadn't known you were due to join the team here at Springfield I would have had you down for a boutique in the town, or a season with the local repertory company.'

'You knew who I was when we met and yet didn't tell me that you were going to be my boss?' she whispered indignantly. 'Why?'

'I don't mix business with pleasure,' he said briefly, and Gaby thought that if he was as low key as that when he was enjoying himself she wouldn't like to see him when he wasn't!

'I would say myocardial infarction,' the GP said after he'd examined the stricken woman. 'We can do an ECG here and take a blood sample to have it checked for enzymes from a damaged heart vessel. Also, Sister Travis will need thrombolytic drugs to get rid of any blood clots.'

'It appears to be a pretty serious attack and it's imperative that any ventricular fibrillation from an irregular heartbeat is avoided. You couldn't have been in a better place for it to happen, Sister,' he told her reassuringly as he took her clammy hand, 'except maybe for the coronary care unit at the Infirmary, and I'm going to get in touch with them once we've got you out of here and onto the ward.'

Ethan Lassiter nodded his agreement and told Gaby crisply, 'Ring for a trolley on the porter's extension, Nurse. Explain that it's urgent.' He gave a wintry smile. 'We might as well make use of you now that you're here.'

As she picked up the phone Gaby nodded without speaking. She was still smarting to think that he'd let her prattle on about herself when they'd met in the churchyard on Saturday and make a fool of herself in the Goose that same evening, when he'd known who she was all the time.

She couldn't understand it. A woman by the name of Joan Jarvis had been hospital manager at Springfield when she'd been offered the vacancy. Where had this guy come from?

He was going to be her boss and she'd already started off on the wrong foot if his aloof manner was anything to go by. Would he have already decided that she was unsuitable before she'd even commenced working at Springfield?

She'd barely had time to replace the phone before a scrawny young male sporting a shaved head appeared with a stretcher trolley, and between them they carefully lifted the sick woman onto it.

Ethan Lassiter glanced at Gaby. 'While Dr Drew and I are seeing to Sister, maybe you could present yourself on the geriatric ward as they'll be one short on there now. Go and introduce yourself and do what you can to assist until I'm free. We're expecting two new admissions on that ward so you can help the other staff to get them settled in. If you follow us I'll point you in the right direction.'

Michael Drew and the porter were already halfway down the corridor and as Gaby and the hospital manager hurried after them he said, 'The fact that we have already made each other's acquaintance is of no consequence as far as I am concerned. I shall be watching how you perform. I'm aware that this is your first post in the health service and you will be given all the assistance you need, but I want to make it clear that the staff at Springfield are all hard-working and dedicated. We're not in the business of playing at medicare. Do I make myself clear?'

Gaby grimaced. She hadn't been wrong about putting her foot in it! 'Yes, sir,' she said meekly. 'Clear as crystal.'

Theirs had been a chance meeting. *He* had behaved with cool politeness, while *she*. . . Her face burned at the thought. She had given him cause to think that she might be in fashion. . .or on the stage. Talk about the actress and the bishop!

To everyone's concern and dismay, Flora Travis, the oldest member of staff at Springfield, *had* suffered a heart attack. Consequently, it was much later in the morning when Gaby received her official welcome to the small community hospital, after making the acquaintance of the other nurses on Geriatric and helping to admit a crotchety old man with pneumonia and a confused elderly lady suffering from diverticulitis.

'Sit down, Nurse Dennison,' Ethan Lassiter said with his cool smile when Gaby appeared in his office in answer to his summons. 'If you didn't know before, I would imagine that by now you'll understand what is meant by the phrase ''being thrown in at the deep end''.'

Her usual beam absent, Gaby managed a tight little smile of her own but there was concern in her dark eyes as she asked, 'How is Sister Travis?'

'Responding to treatment,' she was told, 'but I think that Dr Drew may have her transferred to the coronary unit at the infirmary this afternoon, just to be on the safe side. It was most fortunate that he was in the hospital at that moment. Normally he would have been taking morning surgery but he'd called in to pick up some case notes on his way there.

'I presume that you are aware that the hospital is serviced by a group of GPs, along with regular visits from the consultants. We don't have any resident doctors here.'

Gaby nodded confidently. She had done her homework on the running and functions of a community hospital.

'The GPs consist of Mike Drew and his partner, Peter Abbotsford, along with Bevan Marsland who has just married Sister Bryant, my second in command. We are also served by a couple of GPs from a practice on the outskirts of the town, which is nearer to us than the infirmary.'

'There are two main wards—one for post-operative and non-surgical complaints, which we call the general ward, and the other is for geriatric patients.'

'We also have a small operating theatre and a casualty department. All these varying parts of the hospital are staffed by teams of nurses with accompanying physiotherapists when required. I had thought to put you with the casualty team to begin with but Sister Travis's illness leaves us short on Geriatric and, even though a newly qualified nurse can't be expected to fill the gap left by a very experienced sister, at least you will be an extra pair of hands.'

So much for her hopes of being the reincarnation of Florence Nightingale, she thought ruefully as he waited to see if she had any comments to make. As far as the hospital manager was concerned, her immediate function would be merely as an extra pair of hands but she wasn't going to go down without fighting, and she said innocently, 'I believe it was the wedding of your second in command that I witnessed on Saturday?'

His face tightened. He obviously wasn't expecting *that* sort of a question. 'Yes, it was. Cassandra Bryant and Bevan Marsland met here at Springfield and are now honeymooning at a secret destination. They are very much in love and Cassandra's son, Mark, is also very happy about the match. The older couple representing them were Joan and Bill Jarvis.

'Joan was previously matron manager here but she resigned a couple of months ago when she found she was pregnant. Being somewhat older than the average mother-to-be, she finished working the moment she was sure of the glad tidings. Hence my own arrival to take over the running of the hospital.

'And having said that I *do* have a hospital to run and you a new job to settle into, so if you will proceed back to Geriatric the staff there will continue to help you to find your feet. Needless to say, if you have any problems or difficulties that you can't resolve alone I shall want to hear about them.'

As Gaby made her way back to the ward she was thinking about the wedding scene they'd been discussing. There *had* been a happy radiance about the blonde bride and her bridegroom—and the young boy who'd stood so proudly beside them—and from what the remote hospital manager had just told her the Jarvis couple also had a lot to be joyful about. It had looked to be a happy event for everyone, except the man who had just dismissed her with cool politeness from his office. There'd been no gladness in *his* manner and she was still wondering why.

CHAPTER TWO

BY THE time Gaby got back to Cleeve House that night her mind was overflowing with the day's impressions. Getting to know her new colleagues and the patients, exploring the attractive layout of the hospital, and lastly, but by far the most riveting, had been the discovery that the man she'd met in the churchyard and later in the Goose was the hospital manager at Springfield.

'Ethan Lassiter actually comes from the village,' an auxiliary nurse on the geriatric ward had told Gaby when she'd tried to find out more about him, 'but he's been down south for a few years, working in a similar environment to this. When our matron manager gave in her notice he applied for the job with a view to being back on his own territory.'

'What is he like to work for?' Gaby had asked, with his brusque warning still ringing in her ears.

The other woman, a pleasant, freckle-faced part-timer, had laughed. 'All right, as long as you're male. . .or a female over forty,' and as Gaby had stared at her blankly, she'd continued in a more sepulchral tone, 'We think that some woman has done him wrong.'

'So he's not married?'

'Not unless he's got her hidden away somewhere. He lives alone in one of the nicest houses in the village.'

'He was gazing very pensively at the bride at the wedding on Saturday,' Gaby had told the surprised auxiliary. 'I was standing next to him in the churchyard. Maybe he's suffering from unrequited love.'

It was the other woman's turn to stare. 'No,' she'd said firmly. 'That was Cassie Bryant. She would never encourage another man. She adores Bevan Marsland. Cassie has only ever looked at two men in her life and the other was Bevan's brother, who gave her a child, but *he* has been dead for years.

'Our new hospital manager is a loner,' she'd gone on to say, 'but whatever might be lacking in his personal life, he is certainly on the ball when it comes to health care. Joan Jarvis, his predecessor, was excellent at the job, but Ethan Lassiter's efficiency even puts hers in the shade.'

Gaby had nodded gloomily. It looked as if her first impressions had been right. This Lassiter fellow was no bundle of joy, more like a bale of cold perfection, but at least there was one comfort in it. His lack of interest in her when they'd met hadn't been personal. If what her freckle-faced colleague had just told her was correct he wasn't even likely to warm up if she performed the dance of the seven veils in front of him!

As she'd made up a bed for a new patient being transferred from the infirmary, Gaby had told herself philosophically that she probably wouldn't see much of him if she kept her mind on the job. Ethan Lassiter was hardly likely to be concerning himself overmuch with a minion such as she, even though she had unfortunately brought herself to his notice on two previous occasions.

He'd appeared on the geriatric ward just before Gaby was due to finish, and informed the anxious staff that Sister Travis had been transferred to the coronary unit at the infirmary and that her condition was now stable.

'What about her animals?' one of the staff had asked. 'Flora has a menagerie of stray cats and dogs up at her house. Somebody will have to feed them.'

'I shall see to that myself,' he'd said quietly, 'but as I have no wish to go rummaging through her things, perhaps one of you could arrange to pack some clothes and toiletries for her?'

'I'll do that,' Clare Duncan, one of the SRNs, had offered eagerly. 'Let me know what time you'll be feeding the animals and I'll come round.'

She was small and slim, with provocative blue eyes and a very curvy body, and, watching them, Gaby had thought that it would be interesting to see his reaction to the rather obvious manoeuvre.

'No need for that,' he'd said coolly. 'I'll give you Flora's key and you can let yourself in whenever you want. The animals are all outside and I shall take food for them with me.'

The blonde SRN had pouted and Gaby had thought that the auxiliary she'd chatted with earlier hadn't been far off the mark. Ethan Lassiter would be a hard fish to catch but, then, who wanted to go fishing?

As he'd turned to go she had caught his eye and he'd asked briefly, 'How has your first day gone, Nurse Dennison?'

'Fine, thank you, Mr Lassiter,' she'd said demurely, and had wanted to add, In spite of being given the gipsy's warning before I'd barely set foot in the place.

'Good,' he'd replied distantly, and had gone on his way, leaving her with an insane desire to make him really notice her.

* * *

The next morning she found that she'd been moved to the general ward on Ethan's instructions and, as she helped to settle in the patients who'd been transferred from the orthopaedic unit at the infirmary after surgery, the feeling was still with her.

He had filled the gap left by Flora Travis's illness by moving one of the sisters from Casualty into Geriatrics, which made them fully staffed and left Gaby available for wherever he decided she was needed.

As she helped with the new arrivals her face was solemn. Ethan Lassiter had informed her the previous day that the staff at Springfield weren't playing at health care. Well, neither was she and it annoyed her that he might have thought otherwise.

Just because she was a carefree spirit it didn't mean that she had no sense of responsibility—far from it. Those six months spent in Sorrento at her *nonna's* bedside were not the behaviour of an irresponsible person but, then, neither was she prepared to go around with a face as closed up as his.

She would show him her worth and he would have to admit that he'd made a mistake. Whether he was a misogynist or not she would make him notice her, and then it would be *her* turn to ignore *him*.

Amongst the surgical cases that the infirmary had passed on to Springfield for further care was an attractive twenty-year-old man who had been given an osteotomy. In his case it had entailed the shortening of the bone in a good leg to make it the same length as his other limb, which had been badly fractured and in the process of healing had become shorter than before.

'Dr Lucinda Beckman has done the operation,' one of the other nurses told Gaby. 'She has recently taken over the orthopaedic unit at the infirmary and will follow up his progress while he's here at Springfield. The consultants call in to see their post-operative patients from time to time and there is invariably a GP on the premises during the day, should we need the services of a doctor.'

'What is Dr Beckman like?' Gaby asked, as there'd been something in the other nurse's voice when she'd said the name.

'Brilliant at the job but bossy. . .and a man-chaser. There was no love lost at one time between her and Cassandra Bryant, our sister manager, but I think that they're on better terms now.'

The osteotomy patient was an easy-going man called Dave, with long brown hair tied back in a ponytail and sporting a gold earring. When he saw Gaby's slender curves and her own dark mane fastened back in a similar style to his he joked, 'If you are an example of what the NHS has on offer these days it makes it all worthwhile.'

She smiled. 'Makes what worthwhile?'

'Letting them turn me into a dwarf,' he said with a grin.

As Gaby threw her head back and laughed up at the lofty six feet of him, Ethan Lassiter's voice said from behind, 'When you've finished entertaining the patients, Nurse, maybe you can see to their medical needs.'

Before she could defend herself he had gone on his way, the straight set of his broad shoulders expressing disapproval, and Gaby thought glumly that so far her introduction into health care had gone off like a damp squib.

The new patient was watching her, his eyes apologetic. 'Sorry about that,' he said in a low voice, 'but

I just had to tell you how you've brightened my day.'

'Think nothing of it,' she said airily. 'I'm new here and my boss hasn't had time to realise my true worth.'

'Must be blind, then,' he told her as she helped him to a comfortable chair in the day-room adjoining the ward.

'Blinkered, maybe,' she said quietly, and this time she wasn't laughing.

The hospital manager's office was at the front of the building, and as she passed it on her way home Gaby glanced across briefly and saw Ethan sitting at his desk deep in thought. His face was in shadow but the late afternoon sun was bright on the gold of his hair. For some reason that she couldn't explain Giorgio's face came to mind, with its sensual lips and inviting dark eyes, and there was no pleasure in the memory as she compared it to Ethan Lassiter's Nordic calm.

She'd gone to bed early after her first day at the hospital. What had he occupied himself with on the previous evening, she wondered, apart from feeding Flora's animals? Whatever it was it had nothing to do with her, and the less she let such thoughts take over her mind the better.

That night at dinner her fellow boarders were discussing a sports day that was to be held in the village on the coming Saturday in aid of the hospital and Noah Chaplin, the construction engineer, said jovially, 'It's for the public and any hospital staff who want to take part. So how about it, young lady? Are you going to enter?'

Gaby's face brightened. 'Yes, why not?'

In this her first week she was working from Monday to Friday. It wouldn't always be like that. She would have to do her share of weekend work and so, if there was something happening this coming Saturday, she might as well take the opportunity of getting to know people.

She was happy in her new surroundings. She liked meeting people and they invariably warmed to her bubbly, uncomplicated charm. The nursing staff on the whole were friendly and hard-working. The GPs, as they came and went, didn't pull rank, and Gary, the young porter with the shaved head whom she'd discovered to be a caring husband and father, had already brought photographs of his young daughter to show her.

On top of that Jean Baird, the middle-aged woman in charge of physiotherapy at Springfield, had invited her to her home for dinner one evening and so, all in all, Gaby was happier than she'd been in ages.

It was only when she found herself being observed by a pair of watchful, dark blue eyes that everything didn't seem quite as pleasant as she was telling herself it was, but on those occasions she carried on with her duties and made herself scarce at the same time.

Being a part of the small community hospital meant a lot to her, and by the end of the first day she had known that she liked the close-knit atmosphere of Springfield much more than the impartiality of the big hospital where she'd trained.

In spite of her gregarious nature there had been times when she'd felt lonely there and it had been a thousand times worse during those months in Italy. Her father and Jessica had been more concerned with how much money a promotion of 'three garments cleaned for the price of one' would bring in than how *she* was coping with her sick *nonna* on her own.

But now she was being given the chance to put

down roots, make new friends and become involved in the career that she'd trained for. If there was a fly in the ointment in the shape of Ethan Lassiter, then so be it. She would just have to prove to him that she wasn't a pushy little sexpot.

Although there was the tang of autumn in the air, Saturday dawned a bright, sunny day. The sporting charity event was to take place on the field that, along with the road, separated Springfield from the fast-flowing river.

Some months previously that same river had threatened to burst its banks and flood the hospital but nature, with its capricious moods, had changed its mind at the last moment, to the relief of all concerned.

When Gaby arrived with the rest of the folk from Cleeve House the sideshows and refreshment tent were already filling up with onlookers and prospective participants, and as she looked around her she could pick out the GPs with their families and girlfriends. Even the limp-haired Michael Drew had a brown-eyed girl clinging to his arm and lower down the field were Gary, the porter, and his family.

Gaby had entered for the four hundred metres sprint and one of the organisers inside Springfield had persuaded her to join the hospital's tug of war team.

'You may not carry much weight,' she'd been told laughingly, 'but you'll be good for distracting the other team.'

There was no sign of Ethan Lassiter and yet she knew that with his extreme attention to detail he would be there. . .if only to make sure that no one put a foot wrong, she thought with wry amusement as the start of the four hundred metres was called.

It was when she was lined up with a dozen others

that she saw him, dressed in a blue cotton shirt and white shorts, deep in discussion with the man who was to fire the starting shot. But before she had the chance to observe him further the pistol cracked and they were off.

She had always been able to run, with a fleetness of foot that left others behind. It was the same today and, as her friends from Cleeve House noisily cheered her on, Gaby knew that she was out in front...until she heard heavier feet than hers padding up from behind. As she lunged towards the tape with hand outstretched there was a flash of blue and Ethan Lassiter was there before her.

'I didn't know that *you'd* entered!' she gasped indignantly as he eyed her calmly. 'You weren't in the line-up!'

'Am I to take it that you're accusing me of something?' he asked blandly, without any sign of breathlessness. 'Only if you are, and I really don't see why, I was prevented from lining up with the rest of you by having to deliver a message to the man with the starter pistol. Does that satisfy you? Perhaps I should point out that this is supposed to be a fun event...not the Olympics.'

'Yes, I suppose so,' she agreed reluctantly, aware that she was behaving like an idiot, but with the devil still driving her, she added, 'I would imagine that *you* have to be successful in everything you undertake.'

He'd been eyeing her with tolerant amusement but that remark brought the shutters down again. 'Is that so? Maybe I see *you* as a challenge, then. Someone to be brought into line?'

Gaby felt her cheeks burn. She was alienating him again, and why, for heaven's sake? It wasn't because she was peeved at his lack of interest in her or because she was on the rebound from Giorgio. There were plenty of other fish in the sea who would be only too glad to be hooked if she threw out her line.

It was because she wanted to know this man better. Because irritating though he might be, he was different from anyone she'd known before but whether that was a good thing or not she wasn't sure.

But, whatever reasoning she was coming up with, there was no way she wanted him to see how he was affecting her and so, with a flippancy that didn't come as easily as it might, she told him, 'It will be time to start talking about bringing me into line when I've done something wrong. In the meantime, perhaps we could both remember that it *is* the weekend...that we're not on duty...and are supposed to be here to enjoy ourselves!

'Rest assured that when Monday morning comes round again I shall be wearing my badge of subservience once more but, in the meantime...'

'You have some nerve!' a voice said in her ear as she moved away from him, and Gaby turned to see the freckle-faced nurse that she had met on her first day at Springfield eyeing her in some amazement.

'Nobody, but nobody, gives that sort of cheek to Ethan Lassiter,' she whispered. 'What was it all about?'

Gaby swallowed, tears pricking. 'He just pipped me in the four hundred metres.'

The other woman's amazement increased. 'And that was it?'

'Er...well...no. That was just a side issue. I got off on the wrong foot with him in the beginning and he isn't letting me forget it.'

'From what I've just heard I'd say that you aren't exactly helping matters. Ethan is an excellent boss and, from all accounts, a thoroughly decent man so why should you be at loggerheads with him?'

'I don't know,' Gaby told her dismally. 'I just don't know.'

She left the packed field and went for a solitary walk by the river after that. What the other nurse had said made sense. It would serve her right if she was called in front of a disciplinary hearing for her behaviour this afternoon but, as she'd so acidly pointed out to him, they were off duty and that being so she was free to say what she liked.

But it didn't make her feel any better and she would have gone straight back to Cleeve House if Noah hadn't come looking for her to announce that the tug of war was about to commence.

The two teams were facing each other determinedly when she got there and Gaby tagged herself on at the back of the hospital contestants, who were looking a lot more fit than those from the village.

Peter Abbotsford, one of the GPs, was in front of her and as she clasped him around the waist he said jokingly, 'If the yokels get a look at those long brown legs of yours, Gaby, our victory will be a foregone conclusion.'

It was, and as they pulled their opponents across the line the members of the hospital team went flying backwards in a heap with her beneath them, but only for a second. She was saved from the crush by a pair of broad shoulders ramming themselves in front of her and taking the weight of the falling bodies, and as his eyes met hers Ethan Lassiter said with a sigh, 'Has anyone ever told you that knowing you is a wearing pastime, Gabriella?'

He put his hands beneath her shoulders and brought her carefully upright, and Gaby was aware that her breasts were only a fraction away from his chest and that his touch was a delight that she didn't want to end. She dared not raise her eyes any higher because when they saw his mouth she would want to kiss it and she could imagine the sort of reception *that* would get!

'Thanks for keeping the crush off me,' she told him, twirling a tendril of her long, dark hair between her fingers.

'My pleasure,' he said drily. 'I had to make sure that nothing prevented you from reporting for duty on Monday.' And on that back-to-basics note he departed.

Over Sunday breakfast the next day Gaby asked her youthful landlady where the hospital manager lived and was duly given directions. It was a mellow autumn day again and she decided to go for a brisk walk as the rest of Sally's boarders hadn't yet put in an appearance.

It was no coincidence that she pointed herself in the direction of the house called Higher Reaches and when she found it, beside a straight stretch of the river, she gave a gasp of delight.

Double fronted, with mullioned windows glinting out of golden Cotswold stone, it stood amongst colourful gardens with the green fields of Gloucestershire backing on to them.

As she stood in the shadow of a large tree on the lane outside, Gaby's admiration was tinged with envy and she had a sudden feeling of being lost and alone.

All right, she wasn't exactly homeless but at that moment it seemed as if she was. There was a 'take it, or leave it' sort of place for her with her dad and Jessica above the busy dry cleaners and there *had* been a second home for her in Sorrento, but that had gone for ever and she didn't want the first option.

Ethan Lassiter was a lucky man to live in such a divine house, she thought wistfully, even though he had no one to share it with but, if what she'd been told was correct, that was how he wanted it.

'What's this, then?' his voice said suddenly from behind her and when she turned he was there, with the morning papers under his arm. 'Checking up on me, are you?' he went on as she gazed at him, mesmerised. 'Satisfying yourself that I don't sleep in a filing cabinet in the office?'

The dark blue gaze that seemed to be dominating her every thought these days was taking in the black top and vividly patterned cotton skirt she was wearing over it, while she in turn was enjoying seeing him out of a smart suit for once.

In jeans and a white short-sleeved shirt that showed golden chest hair at the neckline he seemed less formidable, even though his greeting hadn't been without its sting. But this morning she hadn't a flippant answer ready. She was entranced with the house...and even more so with its owner, and knew she was a crazy woman for allowing it to happen.

She was twenty-one, a member of the floating population so to speak, while her boss would easily be in his late thirties, with a very responsible position, a lovely home, and with all the exciting characteristics of the attractive male thrown in—yet she felt that he wasn't happy.

There was a joylessness about him that worried her and, as they stood observing each other, Gaby thought that maybe *she* was the lucky one after all.

Ethan was still waiting for her to answer his droll question and, dragging her thoughts back to what he'd said, she told him truthfully, 'Someone told me that you lived in the nicest house in the village and I thought I'd come and see for myself.'

He raised a surprised eyebrow. 'And?'

'It's lovely,' she said sincerely. 'I'd give anything to live in a house like this...to bring my children up in such a place.'

At her words his face became wiped of all expression and, as he opened the gate and motioned for her to enter the garden, he said offhandedly, 'But you *have* a home, haven't you?'

Her wistfulness gone, Gaby laughed. 'Yes, of sorts, but my father and stepmother are completely absorbed in their dry-cleaning business and my grandmother's home in Sorrento, where I've always spent every spare minute, is no longer there.'

'Why is that?'

Gaby swallowed. 'She died two months ago. That is why I was late in coming into nursing after finishing my training. I spent six months in Italy caring for her after she'd had a stroke.'

'Not entirely on your own, I would hope?' he said incredulously.

'Yes. There *was* no one else. My mother died some years ago.'

His jaw had tightened. 'You are telling me that a bit of a kid like yourself was left to nurse a terminally ill patient over a long period like that?' he asked abruptly.

Gaby turned away. Typical of his type, he wasn't offering sympathy. All he was interested in was getting the ethics of it clear in his mind. It would have been a directive to the area health authority if it had happened in this country or a protest to Social Services that he would be thinking of.

'I am not a bit of a kid,' she said slowly, 'and I can assure you that my *nonna* went nothing short in loving care.'

He tutted irritably. 'Did I say that?'

She shook her head, wishing that she hadn't brought up the subject of her *nonna's* death. Her grief was still very raw, and she didn't want to dissolve into tears in front of Ethan Lassiter.

Maybe he guessed her feelings as, not looking directly at her, he suggested, 'As you're so impressed with the house perhaps you'd like to see round it.'

Gaby felt her colour rise. This was more than she'd bargained for. He was offering to show her around his delightful house and she knew that she wasn't going to refuse.

'I knew that I was coming back to Gloucestershire some months ago and bought this place well in advance,' he said as the heavy oak door swung back to reveal a lofty hallway from which rose a wide curving staircase.

Gaby was looking around her in some amazement. The proportions of the house were delightful but the decor was all wrong. Vivid and oppulent, it clashed with the spacious grace of the lovely old building and as they went from room to room it was the same until they came to the master bedroom which was decorated in pale grey and white.

His bedroom was how she would have expected the rest of the house to be, she thought...cool and understated, like him. As for the other rooms...well!

Ethan Lassiter's eyes had been on her as he'd shown her round and now, as they stood in the doorway of the one room that was in keeping with the house, he asked, 'Well? Does the inside of Higher Reaches match its outer charm?'

Gaby surveyed him with huge dark eyes. How could he ask such a question? He must know that it didn't! But she could hardly tell him so and yet why lie? Ever since their meeting in the churchyard her natural honesty had been asserting itself more than ever and so, unable to tell him a glib untruth, she said, 'This room is perfect...the rest of the house is...er... like...' she paused, searching for a comparison '...like...a...bordello.'

There was a deadly silence as he digested the criticism and then he broke it by asking drily, 'So am I to take it that you are familiar with the inside of such a place?'

Her eyes dancing, Gaby threw back her head and laughed, more in relief than anything else because he hadn't blown his top at the outrageous remark.

'Of course not,' she told him with mock piety. 'I've already explained that my horizons to date have encompassed no more than a busy dry cleaners in Birmingham and a small rented apartment in Sorrento.

'Though if the government can't do any better than the small percentage increase they're offering nurses, I might have to find some way of bolstering my income.'

She thought for a moment that Ethan was going to join her in easy laughter but instead, as if merriment was in short supply in his life, he said, 'The interior decorating of the house was the choice of someone that I was expecting to live here with me and, although I thought it rather garish at the time, I was too fond of her to argue about it.'

He'd offered the explanation as a plain statement of fact, but Gaby sensed a deep hurt behind his words and her amusement was banished by contrition.

She found herself reaching out to touch him and as

she gripped his arm it was there again, the delight of her flesh coming into contact with his. 'I'm sorry,' she said gently. 'It was unforgivable of me to be so rude. What happened? Did she die?'

'Die!' he exclaimed, his jaw slackening in surprise. 'No, of course not. Erica is alive and well, as far as I'm aware. It was the relationship that died.'

'And you've been in mourning ever since,' Gaby commiserated solemnly. 'I saw your expression when you were watching the bride last Saturday. Had *you* planned to get married to this...er...Erica?'

Ethan was closing his bedroom door and moving towards the stairs and, as he waited for her to join him, he said tetchily, 'Yes, I had. It was just a week before the wedding that it all fell apart but don't let your imagination run away with you, Gabriella. I'm not in mourning for anything or anyone. I am merely getting on with my life and if it should be that it doesn't include a member of your sex it is because that's how I want it. Understood?'

'Yes,' she told him meekly, averting her eyes from the scarlet and gold embossed wallpaper above an emerald green dado.

'Good,' he said briskly, as if fending off predatory females was a familiar exercise, 'and now can I offer you some refreshment—tea, coffee, or a glass of wine—before you go on your way?'

'No, thanks,' she told him with a bright smile that hid her deflation and, determined to get a laugh out of him one way or another, she added, 'I would have understood if you'd lived in the filing cabinet after seeing your ex-partner's ideas of decor!'

He did laugh then, a deep, amused rumble from low in his throat, and taking her wrist he drew her into the kitchen. 'At least let me give you a glass of lemonade,' he persisted. 'In honour of the fact that you are my first visitor.'

Gaby stared at him. 'No one has been here since you moved in?'

'No. I've had no wish for company or time for it either. I've been too engrossed with Springfield but when I *do* have a little more time to myself...I shall redecorate.'

She nodded her agreement. 'It's such a lovely house,' she said fervently. 'It would be a shame to spoil it for the lack of a few pastel shades.'

He was handing her a glass of lemonade and as Gaby drank it thirstily he said sombrely, 'I agree but, as we have both perhaps found to our cost, it's the people living in the house that create its ambience... not the colour of the wallpaper.'

'That is so,' she agreed with a lump in her throat and as she put the empty glass down on the worktop there was a strange sensation inside her, like the fluttering of butterflies' wings. Could it be panic? Because she was finding herself attracted to this man against all her normal inclinations?

On the surface he came over as very cool—someone sufficient unto himself—while she was ebullient, tender-hearted and humorous. Yet something was pulling her towards him. Maybe she was looking for an anchor, wanting to put down roots.

If it should be so, it was the first time that she'd felt like that and, in stunned disbelief, it was dawning on her that it would be very easy to fall in love with this strong, quiet man who, after a disastrous love affair, was steering clear of women.

Why couldn't she have met him before it all went wrong, and yet would it have mattered if she had? The chances of the two of them walking pathways to the galaxies was just about nil. They were poles apart in almost everything—personality, outlook and importance. For wasn't *he* the big white chief at Springfield and *she* on the very first rung of the ladder?

CHAPTER THREE

THE bride of two weeks ago was back from her honeymoon, with an air of deep contentment about her that was delightful to see. The tropical sun had bleached her hair to white gold and tanned her fair skin with its rays and, when Gaby met her for the first time, she took an instant liking to Cassandra Marsland, sister-in-charge of Springfield.

'I'm sorry I wasn't here to greet you when you started, Gabriella,' she said when Gaby was summoned to her office on Cassandra's first day back, 'but I'm sure that Mr Lassiter will have kept you under his wing while you've been settling in.'

'Yes, he has,' she agreed wryly, thinking that it had been more a case of being under his eagle eye than his wing.

'And so how's it going?' Cassandra wanted to know.

'Fine, thank you, Sister,' Gaby told her enthusiastically. 'I love it. Everyone has been great and this part of England is so beautiful.'

'Nicer than Sorrento?'

Gaby eyed her in surprise and Cassandra smiled. 'Yes, I've been told that you spent quite some time in Sorrento before coming here. Ethan Lassiter told me and we are both impressed with the task that you undertook out there.'

The colour had drained from Gaby's face at the unexpected introduction of her recent sorrow into the conversation and, seeing it, Cassandra said gently, 'I'm sorry if I've distressed you.'

Her beautiful young face was clearing and her smile flashed out again as she said, 'I'm all right, Sister. Like a lot of people I keep my grief under wraps, and when it's suddenly brought into the light it hurts.'

'Yes, I can understand that,' Cassandra told her, 'and remember, Gabriella, you are young and rather alone, it would seem, so if you ever need a listening ear or a shoulder to cry on, Ethan and I are both here for you.'

Gaby turned away so that the other woman wouldn't see the disbelief in her eyes. She could just see Ethan Lassiter allowing her to make a damp patch on his shoulder. He would be more likely to thrust a tissue at her.

'And now,' Cassandra was saying, 'I think that on this fine morning I should let you get back to the wards, while I catch up on what's been happening during my absence.'

Gaby turned in the doorway. 'I saw your wedding, Sister.'

'You did? How did that come about?'

'I'd just arrived in the village and was coming out of the railway station when I saw what was happening so I stopped to watch. It was lovely!'

She wasn't going to tell Cassandra that she'd met her future boss at the same time and that ever since clapping eyes on him he had never been out of her mind.

Cassandra smiled. 'Did you think so? I know that *I* did but, then, I'm predjudiced. I'm a very lucky woman,' she said dreamily, and for a brief second Gaby felt envy inside her.

Out in the corridor she waylaid an elderly man from

the geriatric ward, who was making his way towards the main exit clad only in dressing-gown and slippers, and as she took his arm Gaby was remembering Ethan's expression that day in the churchyard. He must have really loved this unknown woman who went in for emerald green dados and she would give a lot to know what had gone wrong between them.

As the old man tried to shrug off her hand she asked gently, 'And where are *you* off to, Harry?'

'I'm going home,' he said crustily. 'I've been in this place long enough.'

'But you only arrived yesterday,' she told him placatingly. 'They sent you here from St Cuthbert's after the emergency operation to remove your spleen. The doctors there want you to have a few days with us at Springfield to get over it and have a rest. The registrar who performed the operation will be coming along to see you. It was a very nasty fall you had and the blow you received to your stomach meant that they had to take you down for surgery before your spleen ruptured.'

He eyed her sourly. 'Aye. I know all about that. It was her next door's fault. That tabby of hers had crept up my stairs without me seein' it. It was on the top step an' I went flyin' over it. Came a right cropper!'

Gaby surveyed him compassionately. Life could be so unfair. Here was a typical case of an elderly person who'd been coping with determination and common sense in his day-to-day living, until the unforseen had occurred and jeopardised his fitness and his freedom.

Because even if Harry *hadn't* lost his confidence after this, it would mean that Social Services would be monitoring him to a greater degree than before and there was no telling what lasting effect the operation would have on him as there was always a greater risk of infection to a person after removal of the spleen.

'If you'll come back to the ward with me I'll see you have something special for your tea,' she coaxed. 'What would you like?'

'A couple of savoury ducks,' he said immediately.

Gaby frowned. 'What are they?'

Harry gave a grim chuckle. 'It's obvious that you're not a northerner if you don't know what savoury ducks are. You'd better ask the cook.'

'Er...yes...I... think... I'd...better,' she said, with an uneasy feeling that she'd bitten off more than she could chew—or it might turn out that Harry had!

'Don't make promises that you can't keep, Nurse,' Ethan Lassiter's voice said from the doorway of his office. 'It is one sure way of delaying recovery.'

Her eyes raked his face. Was he kidding? Taking the mickey? Or had her ready tongue got her into trouble again?

'I was merely trying to stop the patient from leaving the hospital of his own accord,' she told him in a low voice. 'I *had* to say something.'

'I see. Well, that being the case, *I* will take the gentleman back to the ward and while I'm doing so you can take his advice.'

'What?'

'Go and work your charms on Cook.'

Gaby groaned silently. Alice Trethowan was a Cornish woman who had never been north of Plymouth. The chances of her knowing what a savoury duck was were remote and the possibility of her leaving the other meals to make it specially for Harry, providing of course that she knew what it was, was even less likely.

'And when you have done that I'd like to see you

in my office,' he said in a tone of voice that told her exactly nothing.

'That will be faggots, I'm thinking, me dear,' Alice said calmly when she explained about her rash promise. 'They're the nearest thing to what the northern folks call "savoury duck".'

Gaby began to laugh. 'So they don't waddle and quack?'

'Absolutely not,' the plump, middle-aged cook assured her as she joined in the laughter.

'And. . .can you serve old Harry with this delectable dish. . .tonight, Alice?' she wheedled.

'For you, Gabriella, yes,' she said, 'but mind that you keep your promises simple in future; no caviar. . . or lobster, eh?'

Planting a kiss on her rosy cheek, Gaby waltzed Alice around the kitchen and as the cook ended up chuckling breathlessly beside the big cooking range they looked up to see Ethan watching them with raised eyebrows.

'Sorry, Mr Lassiter,' Alice gasped, flustered at having been caught acting the fool.

'Don't apologise,' he said. 'I can't imagine that the *Come Dancing* display was *your* idea,' and to Gaby, who was standing to one side wishing that her boss would wear studs in his shoes to announce his approach, 'I presume that you have been using your wiles on Alice?'

'This child is like a breath of fresh air in the place,' Alice told him now that she'd got her breath back. 'Just looking at her must do the patients good and, yes, I think we can manage a faggot for poor Harry.'

Gaby looked away. The last thing she wanted to be called in Ethan Lassiter's hearing was a child, as he'd already let her see on a few occasions that he thought her infantile, and as if he'd read her thoughts he said, 'Perhaps you'd like to change from a fast polka... and do a quickstep along the corridor to my office. Or had you forgotten that I want to see you?'

'No, of course not,' she said, rallying. 'But you *did* tell me to speak to Alice first.'

'And have a quick waltz at the same time?'

'Er...no...not exactly.'

'Right, then, let's get mobile before Sister Marsland sends out a search party for you.'

'Sit down, Nurse Dennison,' he said when they went into his office and, wondering what was coming next, Gaby did as she was told.

'It is normal procedure for me to have a chat with new members of staff when they have been with us for a few weeks,' he said from behind the big oak desk, 'and as, in your case, it seems like a lifetime since you came to us I thought now would be a good opportunity.'

'I've only been at Springfield for two weeks,' she said in faint protest.

He tutted. 'Dear me, is that all? Maybe it seems so much longer because you have a habit of making your presence felt.'

'And what is that supposed to mean?' she asked warily.

'I was merely commenting that you aren't the kind of person to go unnoticed.'

Gaby felt herself go warm. The remark could be a compliment while on the other hand...'I don't do it deliberately!' she exclaimed.

His dark blue gaze was boring into her. 'No, I don't believe you do, but the fact remains that you *are* a disturbing influence.'

Her jaw dropped in dismay. Was he saying that she

wasn't going to fit in at Springfield? That she was the original square peg?

'You're not going to send me away, are you?' she asked desperately, 'because if you'll give me another chance I promise I will stop myself from being so noticeable.'

'And how will you accomplish that?' he asked drily.

'I'll only speak when I'm spoken to, wear thick woollen stockings, a bra with no uplift,' she said, half laughing, half serious, 'and I'll never criticise your decorating again.'

'Alice described you as a breath of fresh air,' he said whimsically. '*I* think of you as a minor hurricane but we're not here to talk about that. What on earth makes you think I am going to dispense with your services? And whatever makes you think you can make yourself less noticeable?'

He got up out of his swivel chair and came to stand beside her. 'When I said that you were a disturbing influence I was referring to your effect on me personally. The comment had nothing to do with your work here, which so far I haven't been able to find fault with, so you can forget the dramatic promises of a new image. For one thing it sounded ghastly.'

His eyes went to her thrusting young breasts inside the blue uniform. 'Especially the bra.'

Taking her hand, he pulled her to her feet. Her eyes were wide and startled as their glances met and he said with harsh urgency, 'You'd better go, Gabriella. We've just established that you're happy here and that I'm not going to ''send you away'', as you so poignantly put it, so back to the ward with you before I...'

He was still holding her hand and Gaby thought that if *this* was how it felt at such a small degree of contact how would it be if they were in each other's arms, naked and passionate?

'Before you what?' she questioned breathlessly.

Ethan let her go then, pushing her away from him in the same gesture, and if there had been a disturbing heat in him before, now it was gone.

He straightened his shoulders as if throwing off some unseen burden and told her flatly, 'I was about to say before I change my mind and have you transferred to some far outpost of the NHS.'

He'd opened the door and was waiting for her to depart and, bewildered and bemused, she went.

Autumn had gone and the first nip of winter was in the air and, as the weeks went by, Gaby was aware of various things. Such as the vital part that Springfield played in the health of the community, the keen budgeting that was required to keep it open and the dedication of the man in charge.

She often wondered about the woman who had turned him into a taciturn workaholic, or maybe that was how he'd always been. She wished she knew but whatever the reason Ethan made it very clear that the job came first.

He rarely socialised and Gaby had almost given up hope of meeting him anywhere other than the hospital when Jean Baird, head of physiotherapy at Springfield, reminded her of the invitation to dinner that she'd made when Gaby first started.

'I'm having a small dinner party on Friday,' she said one morning as she supervised Dr Beckman's patients during a physiotherapy session. 'Would you like to come, Gaby? You'll know most of the folks there, apart from my husband and son, and I know that *they'll* be pleased to meet you.'

'I keep telling my son, Simon, about the gorgeous young nurse who's come to work at Springfield,' she said laughingly, 'and it's on the strength of that he's agreed to forego a night out with his pals.'

'How old is your son?' Gaby asked, only mildly interested.

'Twenty-one, the same age as yourself.'

She hid a smile, wondering what Jean would think if she discovered that the young nurse in question had a very strong yen for an older man. A man who rarely looked the side she was on...because of a busy cottage hospital...a lost love...and the fact that he saw his youthful admirer as 'just a bit of a kid'.

Yet there was nothing childish about her feelings for him. She was twenty-one, a grown woman and beautiful as well. Gaby had never experienced real passion before but there was no doubt in her mind that she was capable of it, very much so. It was too bad that it was going to be all one-sided.

On the afternoon of Jean Baird's dinner party the evening ahead was wiped out of her mind by a distressing event. Gaby was on duty, along with one of the sisters, in the hospital's small casualty department, which was used on a less frequent basis than the bigger and busier unit at the infirmary but was an important part of Springfield just the same.

The other nurse had gone to lunch and Gaby was there alone when a passing motorist brought in an elderly lady who had fallen and hurt her arm on the road outside.

She was shocked, tearful and obviously in pain from her injured arm and, as Gaby gently eased off her cardigan, it was already beginning to swell.

'I'll ring for one of the sisters to come and have a

look at it,' she told the woman reassuringly. 'Just stay seated and we'll have you feeling more comfortable in no time.'

As she turned to pick up the phone quick footsteps sounded behind her and the woman gave a terrified shout. 'My bag!' she cried. 'He's taken my handbag!'

Gaby turned to see a flash of blue jeans and dirty trainers disappearing round the door and rage swept over her. The poor soul was already in shock after the fall and now she'd been robbed in the very place that she'd come to for help.

Even as she was thinking it she was flinging herself after him, moving like lightning through a side door in the corridor and out into the gardens where the man was making a beeline for the road.

He glanced over his shoulder and when he saw her in grim pursuit he increased his speed but he was no match for her. Gaby was fit and she was angry...and she was gaining on him.

'What's up?' asked a young mother, pushing a pram towards the visitors' entrance.

'Thief!' Gaby gasped. 'Get help!'

When she was just a couple of feet behind him he turned suddenly, his hand came out and he swiped her viciously across the face. The force of the blow knocked her off her feet and as she lay sprawling on the grass with blood spurting from above her eyebrow and her nose Gaby heard a scuffle somewhere ahead and Gary's voice bellowed, 'We've got him, Gaby...and the bag!'

She closed her eyes thankfully. The porters must have seen what was happening and had blocked his path from the other end.

When she opened them again Ethan was bending over her, outrage and anxiety in his expression, and the pain in her face was a small price to pay when she saw how upset he was.

'We got him,' she said breathlessly. 'The lady's bag is safe!'

'Yes, that is so,' he agreed tightly as he took in her battered face. Putting his arm beneath her shoulders, he raised her carefully to a sitting position. 'Her bag *is* safe, yes, but what about *her*? She was half out of the chair in a collapsed condition when we got to her— another second and she would have been on the floor.

'Your first duty was to the patient. Thief or no thief, you had no right to leave her. I can do without amateur heroics amongst my staff. Originally we had one patient and now we have two! It is *your* turn to be treated in Casualty and I hope that *you're* not left alone in a shocked condition.'

So much for her joy at his concern over her. She might have known that *she* wasn't the cause of his anguish. It was the reputation of Springfield that he was worried about, not a stupid nurse who'd done the wrong thing again as far as he was concerned.

Shrugging off his supporting arm, she said coldly, 'Thanks a bunch, Mr Lassiter. I suppose I *was* wrong to do what I did but all I could think of at that moment was that a patient was being robbed in the hospital where she'd come for help.

'Perhaps you'd better set me some guidelines, such as what action do I take if murder is being committed? Do I continue giving out the brimstone and treacle, or putting a plaster on a cut? Or what is the procedure if I find someone being sexually assaulted in the hospital? Do I offer them the contraceptive pill?'

'How dare you make light of something as serious as this?' he ground out furiously. 'You've been a thorn in my flesh from the moment I offered to carry your suitcase!'

Gaby's defiance was ebbing away. 'I admit that what I did *was* wrong,' she admitted weakly as her head began to thump and her legs started to tremble, 'and I'm truly sorry. It won't happen again.'

As she began to dab at her face with a tissue she found that her legs weren't just trembling they were buckling beneath her, and the last thing she heard before she sank into blankness was Ethan's voice saying raggedly, 'Gabriella! God! What have I said?'

Gaby's fainting attack didn't last long and as she came back to consciousness it was to find that Ethan had swung her up into his arms and was taking her back inside.

Cassandra was coming along the corridor and when she saw them she increased her pace, asking anxiously, 'What's happened, Ethan? Has Gaby had an accident?'

'No. She was hit in the face trying to stop a thieving young thug,' he gritted, 'and she fainted.'

The blonde sister grimaced. 'I've been at the other side of the building and had no idea that all this was going on. We'd better get her into Casualty.'

'That is my intention,' he said in the same tight voice, as he strode towards one of the cubicles, but Gaby wasn't listening. She was looking around her for the patient that she'd left to her own devices while she chased the thief.

'One of the other nurses will be attending to her,' he said before she could ask.

'And I'll take care of *you*, Gaby,' Cassandra said briskly as Ethan put her down carefully on to the bed.

She nodded numbly, bereft of speech. When Ethan had berated her out there in the hospital gardens she'd answered him back with a spate of words that had poured forth without effort but now she was dumb, drained of sense and feeling except for a painful throbbing of the temples—and all because she'd wanted to see the wrongdoer caught and punished.

He stood by impassively as Cassandra cleaned the blood off her face and made no comment when she said commiseratingly, 'You'll have a lovely black eye in a couple of hours' time, Gaby. Witch hazel or cold compresses should bring some of the bruising out but you'll still have a shiner, I'm afraid.'

Gaby sighed. She wasn't bothered about the black eye. She was bruised enough inwardly, so a few discolorations on the outside wouldn't make much difference, she thought glumly.

The phone rang at that moment and, to her relief, Ethan was called away, but not before he'd said, 'An X-ray of the cheek-bone and forehead, don't you think, Sister?' and Cassandra had nodded in agreement.

As they waited to see the plates Gaby was thinking that his disapproval, if it *was* still directed at her, was like an explosive element in the atmosphere and she longed to get away from it.

To her relief they didn't show up any fractures and as she lay back against the pillows of the cubicle Cassandra said, 'So tell me exactly what happened.'

'I left a patient on her own while I chased the man who had stolen her bag,' she explained with grave, youthful honesty.

'And?'

'Ethan. . . Mr Lassiter. . .gave me a ticking-off; said I should have stayed with her.'

'And of course he's right,' the sister-in-charge told her gently. 'I can understand the way you felt. I'd probably have acted in the same way but I'd have been wrong, just like you were, and also, Gaby, you have to remember that he is responsible for your safety while you're working. He would be horrified if one of his staff came to grief while on the job. I think his anger was understandable.'

She sighed. 'Yes, I suppose you're right, but why do I have the feeling that he wouldn't have been so furious if it had been someone else who'd done it?'

'I think you're imagining that,' Cassandra said with a smile. 'He's probably more protective towards you because you haven't any folks around and because you're new here.'

'Protective!' she hooted. 'He's as good as told me I'm a pain in the neck.'

'There are much worse places to have a pain than in the neck,' Cassandra said with a smile, 'and now I think you should go home. You've had a nasty blow to the face and should rest for a few hours. I'm going to find an ambulance to take you back to Cleeve House.'

Gaby had told her young landlady that she would be dining out that evening, but when Sally saw her face as she got out of the ambulance she exclaimed in horror, 'Gaby! Whatever has happened?'

'I was trying to be *Crimewatch UK* all on my own,' she said wryly, 'and got a thump in the face for my efforts.'

'Come into the kitchen and I'll make you a cup of tea,' Sally offered, 'and you can tell me all about it.'

'And you got into trouble for doing that!' she said in surprise when Gaby had finished describing the attack by the thief.

'Mmm. I did,' she said glumly as she drank the mug of hot sweet tea, 'and, to be perfectly honest, Sally, I deserved it as the patient could have had a heart attack or collapsed onto the floor while I was doing my fastest sprint ever.'

'You can hardly be blamed for trying to get her property back though, can you?'

Gaby shrugged. 'I suppose there are two ways of looking at it and I can assure you that my boss certainly didn't see it *my* way.'

'What about tonight?' Sally asked as she eyed Gaby's bruised and swollen face.

'I shall still go,' she said determinedly. 'I don't get so many invitations that I can pass one by. I'll keep bathing my face for the rest of the afternoon and will be generous with my make-up when I'm getting ready for the dinner party.'

She giggled. 'My hostess has a twenty-one-year-old son who has been told of my raving beauty so he's in for a disappointment and as for the rest of those there, they'll have to take me as they find me.'

'Wait while Noah hears about this,' Sally said. 'He'll be livid when he knows what's happened. He likes to think he's keeping a fatherly eye on you.'

'Yes, I know,' she agreed sombrely. 'He's a love. He cares about me more than my own father and as for Ethan Lassiter, my boss...' Her voice faltered at the memory of his anger, and yet had she dreamt that he'd been beside himself with contrition when she'd flaked out?

If he *had* been, it would most likely have stemmed from remorse as much as anything—for having shown her no sympathy when she was hurt. He'd held her in his arms, though, hadn't he, in spite of his annoyance, and being so close to him had made her realise more than ever how he affected her.

'You were saying...?' Sally prompted.

'Er...what?' she asked absently.

'You were about to make some sort of comment about your boss.'

'Oh, yes... Ethan. I was about to say that all *he* was concerned about was the functioning of his beloved hospital and the fact that a gauche young nurse had boobed.'

Gaby had decided to wear white for the dinner party, a full-skirted sleeveless dress that emphasised her smooth brown skin, and as she clutched a small black evening bag and eased herself into strappy sandals of the same colour she was beginning to liven up.

She'd intended sweeping her hair up into a tangled coronet on top of her head and setting it off with long pendent earrings but, in view of the black eye, she'd changed her mind and left the dark mass of her hair hanging loose to cover the bruising.

In spite of her discoloured face the image that gazed back at her from the mirror was one of youthful beauty and allure. Yet she was still a virgin. Neither Giorgio nor any other man she'd met had been able to persuade her to give her body lightly and she wondered in her heart of hearts if she'd been saving herself for just one man. A man who thought her frivolous and flippant... and incompetent, too.

Jean Baird had exaggerated somewhat when she'd told Gaby that she would know most of the people at her dinner party. It turned out that there were three people there that she knew.

One of them was her hostess and the others were Cassandra and her husband Bevan who was one of the GPs at Springfield. Among the people that she knew of, but hadn't yet met, were Jean's husband and her lanky, laid-back son, Simon, and, sitting alongside them, Joan and Bill Jarvis, who in their middle age were to become parents for the first time.

It made eight of them in all, and after there had been general commiseration regarding her injured face the ex-matron manager of Springfield engaged Gaby in general chit-chat about the hospital and her background away from it.

The young staff nurse found her to be a bustling, pleasant sort of woman who was six months into her pregnancy and still somewhat amazed that it was so.

Her bluff, red-faced husband obviously doted on her, and as Gaby watched them together and saw how much Bevan and Cassandra adored each other she was glad that the uninspiring Simon was there to balance the numbers out.

The table was set with fine china and heavy silver cutlery...and there were nine places. As she tried to figure it out, Gaby had her answer. The door opened and Ethan came into the room.

He looked crisp and clean and wholesome in a dark blue blazer, white shirt and grey trousers and he was smiling for once—until he saw her watching him from a seat in the far corner of the room with the Bairds' son draped on the arm of her chair.

Linking her arm in his, Jean said warmly, 'Look who's here, folks. I've persuaded our local recluse to join us.'

Breaking into the chorus of welcoming laughter, he said easily, 'Yes, I suppose that is what I've become of late but I'm like the vampire—I do come out after dark.'

When Simon left her side to assist his father with the wines, Ethan took his place on the arm of her chair with a casualness that fooled everyone except Gaby.

'I've been to Cleeve House to check that you were

all right,' he said in a low voice, 'only to discover that you'd rallied and made your way here.'

'Yes, that is so,' she said, just as quietly. 'I'll bet it's spoiled your night finding out that *I* was going to be here.'

'Is that really what you think?' he said irritably. 'Because if you are so convinced that I can't stand your company—'

'Yes?' she interrupted. 'And if I am...who is to blame?'

'Would you please let me finish?'

'Go ahead.'

'As I was saying, if you are so convinced that I can't stand your company I suppose there is no point in my asking your advice?'

'My advice?' she hooted. 'That'll be the day! Since when have *I* ever said anything of value?'

'When you told me that the inside of my house was like a bordello.'

'Ah, yes, that. Well, I was out of order and I *did* apologise.'

'Yes, you did and, as a follow-up to that, are you going to advise me on how it *should* be done?'

Her eyes were huge in her bruised face. 'You're kidding!'

'I think you know me well enough by now to know that I always mean what I say, Gabriella. Shall we say tomorrow morning for our first consultation?'

His glance switched to Simon, who was scowling at him from the other side of the room. 'That is, unless you have other things to do?'

'Not with Simon Baird,' she told him quickly. 'We only met half an hour ago. Even *I* don't make conquests as quickly as that.'

'Oh, no?'

'What do you mean?'

'Well, it didn't take you long to offload your case onto me that day in the churchyard, did it? That was when I christened you the baggage with the baggage.'

'And were you proved right?'

'Yes, up to a point.'

The sparring between them was brought to an end by Jean calling them to the table and, as Ethan seated himself beside Cassandra—with Joan and Bill Jarvis at the other side of him—Gaby was left to slot herself into the empty seat next to Simon.

'You seem to be very pally with Lassiter,' he muttered as he passed her the vegetables. 'You need to watch it. I heard Mum say that he gave his last girlfriend the heave-ho just before the wedding and he's a bit old for you, isn't he?'

Gaby eyed him stonily. The last thing she felt like doing was defending her boss against this youth but, feeling that she must, she told him airily, 'Not at all. I prefer mature men and, as far as I'm concerned, I feel that it's far better to call off a relationship at whatever time than embark on a loveless marriage.'

She wasn't going to tell Simon Baird that she'd been under the impression that Ethan was the one who'd been jilted—that he was bitter at the loss of the unknown Erica and consequently had adopted the attitude of once bitten, twice shy.

CHAPTER FOUR

THE food was well cooked and appetising and the atmosphere friendly and relaxed, yet Gaby felt on edge. It was a mixture of torture and delight to be in Ethan's company. She longed to be on better terms with him and yet was damned if she was going to crawl.

For his part, he seemed to be totally relaxed now that the evening had got under way and amazingly he hadn't mentioned Springfield once. But Joan Jarvis was about to remedy that.

'Have you any plans of your own for the hospital, Ethan?' she asked during the meal. 'Any special projects in hand?'

'There are a few things that I'd like to accomplish,' he told her, taking his eyes off Gaby and Simon who were toasting each other with brimming wine glasses. 'I've asked the estates department of the Trust to draw up plans and provide quotations for having one of the big store-rooms converted into an assessment flat. It would be for patients whose illnesses restrict them from going back into the community immediately after their time spent in one of our wards.

'If it's going to cost less than twenty thousand I'll have to fund it from my own budget, with the help of whatever fund-raising I can instigate, but should the cost be higher than that then I'm going to have to negotiate with the finance manager of the Trust.'

'That is an excellent idea,' Joan said approvingly. 'Isn't it, Cassie?'

'It certainly is,' the sister-in-charge agreed.

These were the people who would appreciate and understand what he had in mind, Gaby thought, and yet why was it her that he'd been looking at whilst he'd been speaking? Surely *her* opinion wasn't of any importance, but she would be ready with it should he ask for it.

She thought it a marvellous idea that there should be somewhere for the sick to gather their faculties and strength before going back into the often uncaring world outside.

'Also,' Ethan was continuing in his brisk, controlled voice, 'I would like to see some of the rooms in Springfield with *en suite* bathrooms but I'm only too aware that I must walk before I can run. As always, money and red tape are the stumbling blocks. Once one has got clear of those the way ahead opens up and so if anyone here has any ideas for fund-raising I'll be only too pleased to hear them.'

'How about a Christmas Fayre?' Joan suggested.

'Or a bonfire night party?' from Cassandra.

'What about the hospital doing a sponsored walk or swim?' Bevan suggested.

'Or a sponsored kiss?' Gaby suggested dreamily as the wine began to take effect.

That caused a ripple of amusement and, trying to be casual, Simon said, 'Did you have anybody in mind?'

She laughed, her dark eyes dancing in the lamplight. 'It would depend on who's offering,' she told him lightly, avoiding the dark blue gaze that seemed as if it saw into her very soul.

That was the end of the subject and for the rest of the evening she endured Simon's company, feeling more exhausted by the minute as the day's earlier trauma began to take its toll on her spirits and vitality.

By half-past ten Gaby knew that if she didn't leave she would be past making a dignified departure and so she told Jean and her husband regretfully, 'I'm afraid that this afternoon's episode must have taken it out of me more than I thought. Would you mind if I leave? I'd hate to flake out on you.'

'Yes, of course,' Jean agreed. 'It will be delayed reaction that's affecting you, Gaby.'

'And if you still feel unwell tomorrow get one of the GPS out,' Cassandra said. 'Ethan will be looking at security the first chance he gets. He's already been on to the area health authority, as it would seem that monitors in the wards and on the corridors are still not enough to deter sneak thieves.'

Ethan had been out to his car to get a leaflet that Joan had professed interest in and came in on the tail-end of the conversation.

'What's wrong?' he asked immediately, his eyes on Gaby's pale face.

'Gaby isn't feeling too good,' Jean explained. 'I'll get Simon to drive her home.'

He waved his hand dismissively. 'That won't be necessary, Jean. *I'll* take her back to Cleeve House and hand her over to Sally.'

When they went out into the dark, starless night Gaby said wearily, 'Do you *have* to discuss me as if I'm some sort of package requiring delivery?'

She could see the outline of his face but not the expression on it as he said, 'Yes, possibly I do...a sturdy item of merchandise that has suddenly become fragile. You would have been more sensible to have stayed in tonight.'

'What? Staring at the four walls?' she said miserably, as treacherous tears pricked her eyes. 'I've had plenty of experience of that.'

'You could have sat with your men friends at Cleeve House. You seem to be on extremely friendly terms with them.'

'Yes, I am,' she said listlessly, 'and that's what they are—just friendly acquaintances. I soon make friends because I like people and they usually like me but *you* seem to be in a different category.'

'Get in the car,' he ordered quietly, 'and then you can tell me what all this is about.'

When she'd hunched herself in the seat beside him he handed her a big handkerchief and, observing her crumpled face, he probed, 'This is more than the aftereffects of this afternoon, isn't it, Gabriella?'

She gave a sniffle into the clean white square. 'I don't know. It might be because even though I had a lovely time at the Bairds I couldn't help being envious of the happiness that Cassandra and her delightful Bevan have found for themselves and of the contentment of the other two couples, Joan and Bill Jarvis and the Bairds.'

He raised a disbelieving eyebrow. 'But you *are* only twenty-one and you *did* have the attentive Simon hovering all the time.'

'So what? He's not my type.'

He ignored that. 'And what about me?' he questioned. '*I* wasn't throwing a wobbler because I had no partner.'

'No, but, if what I've heard is correct, that's your own fault.'

There was a cold silence in the car and Gaby's dejection increased. Why couldn't she keep her mouth shut? The moment she began to make any kind of impact on Ethan she ruined it by saying something stupid.

'Perhaps you'd like to tell me what you've heard,' he said with level steeliness.

'Er...well...somebody said that you'd jilted your fiancée just a week before the wedding.'

'Did they now? It's amazing how one's past always catches up with one, isn't it? I was living in Surrey at the time, but it's obvious that the NHS grapevine spans the counties.'

'So it's true?'

He sighed. 'Yes, it is true, Gabriella. I called off the wedding just a week before.'

'Why?' It was none of her business but she had to ask.

He was starting the car, and as he eased it out onto the road he said grimly, 'Let's just say that I had a very good reason.'

'And has it put you off women for good?'

To her relief, laughter rumbled in his throat as he told her, 'If it hadn't, meeting *you* would have done the trick.'

If she'd been feeling her normal self she would have joined in his laughter but she wasn't and, to her everlasting shame, Gaby started to cry, great, gulping sobs that had him eyeing her in immediate concern.

He stopped the car, with Cleeve House only a hundred yards further along the road, and, reaching across, put his fingers under her chin and turned her wet face to his. 'Surely you're not crying at what I've just said,' he chided softly. 'I thought you were supposed to be a little toughie.'

'I am!' she gulped. 'But not tonight! What's wrong with me? What is it about me that you don't like?'

He raised his eyes heavenwards. 'You're taking what was just a joking remark completely out of context. As a matter of fact there isn't anything about you that I don't like, except perhaps how you always have to know the top and bottom of every subject under the sun.'

She managed a watery smile. 'So you *do* approve of me?'

His eyes were only inches away and his hand still under her chin as he told her, 'Approval and liking are two different things. I didn't say I approved of you. For one thing, as I've told you before, you're too damned disturbing. Aren't there any men already in your life, Gabriella? Surely there must be.'

She was gazing at him angrily. What was that supposed to mean? He would prefer it if some other man had a claim on her? If she was out of reach? Well, that would be easy enough to contrive.

'There's Giorgio, my Italian boyfriend.'

She'd no intention of explaining that he was married and had recently become a father...but would still like her to be his bit on the side.

'We spent a lot of time together in London when we were training.'

'You mean to say that he's in medicine too?'

'No. He's in the hotel business. He works for his father in Sorrento.'

'What does he do?'

With a picture in her mind of how the conceited Giorgio would look if he could hear what was coming next, she said, 'He's a waiter. He wears a gleaming white coat and Brylcreem on his dark wavy hair... and he smells of...er...lasagne.'

In the shadowed interior of the car Ethan's face was expressionless. 'So you don't see much of him?'

Gaby was well into the part now. If Ethan wanted her to be spoken for so be it, and she gave a heart-rending sigh. 'No. We both have our careers to think of.'

'Hmm,' he said doubtfully. 'How old is this guy?'

'Forty-five,' she said demurely, laying it on with a trowel.

'Good God, Gabriella!' he exclaimed. 'He's older than I am!'

'Yes, I know. But you see, Ethan, it's his maturity that appeals to me.'

'Is that so?' he commented drily. 'And you think I believed all that pollywoddle you've just been feeding me? I suppose next thing you'll be telling me that's why you've been weeping...because you're missing this Giorgio fellow?'

Gaby shook her head. 'No. I was miserable because I'm tired...and envious of people whose lives are full of those who love them.'

'So there isn't a Giorgio?'

'There was but he married somebody else whose parents are wealthy, whereas mine...'

He held up his hand. 'I know; don't say it. They have a dry-cleaning business in Birmingham.'

She was drooping in the seat like a tired flower now that the silly little charade was over, and he said softly, 'It's time you were in bed. You've had quite a day.'

'Mmm,' she agreed sleepily, and then, 'Please say it again.'

'What?'

'That you like me.'

He leaned towards her. 'I like you, Gabriella Dennison. I like you a lot, and I don't particularly want to as you're too beautiful for your own good.'

Gaby closed her eyes and pursed her lips. 'Kiss me, Ethan,' she whispered, 'so that just for a second *I* can feel cherished too.'

He groaned softly and, with her eyes still closed, Gaby waited. Then his mouth was on hers, not gently as she'd expected it to be but fierce and demanding—bringing her into complete wakefulness—and as the heat of their contact warmed her blood she had never felt so wanted in the whole of her life.

Until he put her away from him with a gentleness that hadn't been in his kiss, and said, 'I'm supposed to be looking after your welfare; getting you home safely. Will you please stop playing the temptress, Gabriella? Whatever sort of chaos *your* life might be in . . .*I* know exactly where *I'm* going.'

'And there isn't room on board for me?' she said flatly.

If Ethan had intended answering her, he didn't get the chance. Noah, Hank, the American, and the quiet schoolteacher were coming towards them along the pavement on their way home from the Goose.

'Here's your fan club,' he said quietly, reaching across her to open the car door. 'I'll let *them* see you safely inside.' He touched her cheek for a fleeting second and said gravely, 'Goodnight, Gabriella.'

A glass of Ovaltine from a sympathetic Sally and the banishment from her thoughts of all the downside parts of the time spent in the car with Ethan set Gaby on course for a good night's sleep.

When she awoke to pale winter sunlight the first thing that came to mind was those moments in Ethan's arms when he'd kissed her with a fierce, possessive sort of desperation and then immediately wiped out her rapture by turfing her out of the car to join the other boarders from Cleeve House.

She felt better this morning in every way. The depression of the previous night had gone and her vitality was back. The only thing that hadn't improved was the state of her face. The discoloration was twenty times worse than when the assault had first taken place and as she snuggled under the bedclothes Gaby thought that she was sporting a colour scheme of her own today, in various shades of purple, orange, and brown.

And on that thought came the reminder of Ethan's request of the previous night. Of course she would be delighted to help him choose the right colours for his beautiful house. Anybody wanting scarlet walls with an emerald dado deserved to be jilted. He'd informed her grimly that he'd had a very good reason for doing it, and she had a strong feeling that he wasn't going to divulge it...ever.

When she'd joined Noah Chaplin and his fellow boarders outside Cleeve House the previous night he had been just as incensed as Sally had predicted he would be.

'The cowardly young thug!' he'd growled when he saw her face. 'I'd like to get my hands on him! It was a spunky thing to do, girlie, but it's risky trying to apprehend a criminal these days unless you've a body like mine or Arnold Schwarzenegger's.'

She'd given him a tired smile and told him, 'Everybody keeps telling me that I should have stayed put, Noah, but I'm more for action than caution.'

It was true in more ways than one. Hadn't she manoeuvred some action between Ethan and herself just a short time ago? There'd been no caution in her then, just a mad urge to break down his restraint— and she'd done it.

Whether she would be able to look him in the eye again when next they met was another matter but whatever happened she'd no regrets and as she went down to join the others for breakfast she wondered if he would keep to the arrangement they'd made the previous night that she should help him choose a new colour scheme for his house.

She should have known that he wouldn't forget. At half-past ten Sally showed him into the sitting-room where Gaby was leafing through a magazine and as her heart leapt at the sight of him she thought that he probably never forgot anything and, that being so, it was understandable that she grated on him at times with her less serious approach to life.

'How are you this morning?' he asked as he strode across the room to examine her face.

'Battered but unbowed,' she told him with a smile, as pleasure rocketed through her.

'You slept?'

'Like a baby.'

'Good.' He held out his hand and when she took it he brought her to her feet. 'Let's go, then. I've been into town and got some colour charts.'

'So you're serious? It's not a trap to lure me into your den?'

'I thought we'd dispensed with the bordello comparison, and in any case I'm under the impression that *you* are the one who sets the traps.'

Gaby felt her face warm as she remembered herself saying dreamily, 'Kiss me, Ethan,' and he had, with a thoroughness that had taken her breath away.

'Yes, that's me—the Gloucestershire poacher,' she said breezily, 'and as the catch has been caught once before I wasn't sure whether he'd want a repeat performance.'

As they walked through the village together, the broad-shouldered man with flaxen hair and the slender girl with her long dark tresses, Ethan was greeted by various members of the small community, bustling to and fro as they did their weekend shopping, and there were a few curious glances at his companion.

'Do they know you from when you lived here before?' Gabriella asked. 'Or have they got to know who you are through the hospital?'

'A bit of both, I suppose,' he said easily. 'I was brought up in these parts but a lot of the people I used to know have either died or moved elsewhere.'

'Why did you want to come back?' she asked. 'Was it because the place down south held bad memories?'

He gave a dry smile. 'You always follow one question with another. You'd make a good attorney. Here's your answer. Yes, my surroundings in the south did have some bad memories while this Gloucestershire village has only good ones.'

'Where are your family?' she questioned.

'I haven't got any. My father died when I was twelve and my mother a couple of years ago.'

'So *you* have no one to cherish you either,' she remarked, remembering her lapse into self-pity the previous night, and she was consumed with the urge to tell him that *she'd* be only too willing to fill the gap in his affections.

As Springfield loomed up ahead of them Ethan said, 'I have to call in at my office for some paperwork that I'm going to be working on over the weekend. Do you mind?'

'No, of course not,' she replied. 'Perhaps you would show me the area that you hope to turn into a flat.'

'Yes, of course,' he said immediately. 'I'll be only too pleased. It's good to see that you're interested.'

'I'm interested in most things,' she told him smilingly. 'I've got an enquiring mind.'

'I *have* noticed.'

The store-room that he had in mind for conversion

into a flat was at the back of the building. It had windows on two sides and would easily lend itself to being partitioned. It was only half-full and Gaby asked, 'What do you propose doing with its contents?'

Ethan answered, 'There is the old porter's room in the basement. The stuff can go down there.'

'Do you think there will be any problem getting permission from the powers that be?'

'No, not really,' he informed her. 'It will be financing the venture that will be the problem. I'll have to get in touch with the Friends of Springfield Hospital to see what they can come up with.'

'What about a carnival?' Gaby suggested, steering clear of her suggestion of the previous night.

'So you've abandoned the idea of the sponsored kiss? Young Simon Baird *will* be disappointed.'

'Tough,' she said unfeelingly as the memory of an unsponsored kiss made her body warm.

It was quiet and isolated in the store-room far away from the bustle of the hospital and when he said in a low voice, 'About last night, Gabriella,' her head came up defiantly.

'Yes. What about it?'

'Business and pleasure don't mix. I should have had more sense, even though you issued the invitation.'

'So you *are* prepared to admit that it was a pleasure?' she said unsmilingly, her rosy imaginings of it being the start of their relationship disappearing into the mist.

'Of course it was a pleasure,' he said deep in his throat. 'I'm not made of stone.'

'No?' she questioned with mischievous innocence.

'No!' he gritted as he stepped forward and gripped her shoulders. 'I've as much fire in my bones as the

next man but it's not been kindling much of late...
that is, until *you* came along.'

'And?' she asked, her dark eyes challenging.

'At this moment it's rapidly approaching white heat
and you could get burnt.'

He was drawing her towards him as if it were his
divine right to hold her, as if she were his property,
and Gaby had no argument with that.

It was more than a kiss this time. As Ethan's mouth
covered her parted lips his hands were caressing her
spine and the tempting rise of her slim buttocks and,
from there, cupping the taut globes of her breasts
through the long silk shirt she was wearing.

Their breath was mingling, their desire spiralling,
and as Gaby gasped out her ecstasy she was brought
to earth by the ear-splitting clanging of the hospital's
fire alarm.

'What the dickens is that?' he said with a bemused
groan as he tore himself away from her.

'It's the fire alarm,' she said, collapsing into weak
laughter against the wall. 'We've set it off. The white
heat that you mentioned has caused its own com-
bustion.'

Ethan's eyes were glazed as he moved towards the
passage outside and, recovering, she followed him. If
there *was* a fire it could mean danger and there would
be other things to think about than their need of
each other.

By the time they got to the wards the alarm bell
had stopped and Cassandra, who was on weekend duty,
told him, 'It was a mistake, Ethan. There *was* a small
blaze in a waste bin in one of the corridors. Someone
had thrown the lighted end of a cigarette into it and
an over-zealous cleaner set off the alarm.'

She eyed Gaby's flushed face and asked, 'How do you both come to be here?'

'Er...we were passing,' he said, 'and I stopped off to show Gabriella which part of the building I'd thought to have made into an assessment flat.'

'I see,' she said meaningly. 'And now?'

'She's going to help me choose a new colour scheme for my house.'

Cassandra was observing a woman in her forties making her way slowly and painfully along the corridor towards them with her foot in plaster as she said, 'I thought you had it decorated before you moved in?'

'Yes, I did,' he admitted calmly, 'but the colours were someone else's choice and that person isn't likely to ever live there now. Springfield's newest member of staff thinks she can do better so I'm giving her the chance.'

Gaby was wondering what Cassandra's reaction would be if she was to discover that they'd been in each other's arms when the fire alarm had sounded. Her face was still red but Ethan hadn't batted an eyelid when his second-in-command had queried why they were there.

'We've had a glut of Lucinda Beckman's patients admitted this morning,' Cassandra told Ethan as her mind switched back to hospital matters, 'and this lady is one of them.'

'What's her problem?' he asked.

'Dr Beckman has done a displacement osteotomy on a bunion. She'll be in plaster for some weeks, and as there is a tendency to neglect herself, due to her living alone, Social Services have arranged for her to come to Springfield for a short period of post-operative care.'

'And the rest? The same list that came through the other day?' he questioned.

'Mmm. No changes,' Cassandra told him, 'but you're supposed to be off duty.'

'Yes, I know. I came to get some paperwork that I want to go over during the weekend. I'll only be a moment,' he told Gaby as he went into his office.

'I don't know what you've done to our hospital manager,' Cassandra said in a low voice when he'd gone, 'but he's almost human these days.'

Gaby could have told her that he *was* human... very much so. That she had sure and certain proof of it but whether his feelings were as deep as hers she didn't know, as both times they'd found themselves in each other's arms it had ended with an anticlimax rather than a climax.

She was looking forward to visiting Higher Reaches again and as they walked the short distance, with the river bustling along beside them, Gaby found herself talking about everything under the sun—with the exception of what had happened in the deserted storeroom and Ethan made no attempt to bring those few magic moments into the conversation either.

When the golden stone of the house came into sight Gaby found herself gasping at its beauty again and at her side Ethan was doing the same, but it was amazement that was taking *his* breath away.

There was a car parked outside. It was gleaming white with an open top, and leaning against it was a woman with the same colouring as herself. She was small and of such a brittle slimness that it seemed as if a puff of wind would blow her away.

Her dark hair hung long on her shoulders but the eyes weren't the same as hers. They were grey as the sea on a sunless day.

'Hello, Ethan,' she said in a husky voice. 'Surprised to see me?'

As Gaby watched the unexpected tableau it seemed as if Ethan had withdrawn into some sort of an inner shell as he said flatly, 'What brings *you* here, Erica?'

Erica! she thought in amazement. This was the jilted bride!

Why had she come back? And even as Gaby thought it the petite brunette laughed.

'I could say that it's *you* that's brought me here but you wouldn't like that, would you, Ethan? Your cast-offs reappearing?'

'Why don't you just answer the question?' he said, not rising to the bait. 'But before you do allow me to introduce Gabriella Dennison. She is one of the nurses from Springfield Hospital.'

'And my replacement?'

'Not necessarily. But I'm waiting for you to tell me why you're here. Why you've come all the way from Sussex to make small talk.'

Gaby turned away. This was embarrassing, in more ways than one. He'd been quick enough to let Madam Grey Eyes know that *she* wasn't Erica's successor so maybe he still cared, and yet there was no warmth in his voice for the new arrival—far from it.

'I'm merely passing through,' she told him, 'and thought that you might at least offer me some refreshment.'

'Yes, of course,' he said stiffly. 'Come inside,' and as Gaby opened her mouth to tell him that she would see him some other time, he said, 'I've asked Gaby round to help me choose a new colour scheme for inside the house.'

'Why? Is she going to be living here?' the other woman said sneeringly.

Gaby held her breath. It would be interesting to see what he came up with in answer to *that*.

'Not unless she gets thrown out of her lodgings,' he said with an edge to his voice, 'but my affairs are no longer any concern of yours, Erica. So if you're coming inside for some refreshment, please do so.'

In the pause that followed Gaby managed to get *her* bit in. 'I'll be off, Ethan. Sally will be serving lunch in half an hour.'

It wasn't strictly true. It would be a good hour before there were any signs of lunch at Cleeve House but she couldn't hang on here with Ethan's ex-fiancée strutting about the place as if she still had a share in it.

Even so, she half hoped that he would urge her not to go but he didn't. He dredged up an absent sort of smile and said, 'Sure, Gabriella. Enjoy the rest of the day,' and she was dismissed.

She was scowling as she walked back through the village. Enjoy the rest of the day, he'd said. In whatever way she might spend the rest of it, nothing could compare to those minutes in the storeroom and afterwards she'd been walking on air—until they'd got to his house.

With the appearance of the seductive-looking Erica it had all been spoilt and the more she thought about it the more she was convinced that, on his ex-fiancée's part at least, it wouldn't take much to make the embers spark again.

Her gloom wasn't lightened when she remembered that Noah had gone home to his family for the weekend and, with the feeling that the day couldn't get much worse, she gave in to the suggestion of the other two boarders that they spend the afternoon playing Scrabble.

The evening brought no further sign of Ethan, and

as Gaby was resigning herself to an early night Sally and her husband arrived back from visiting a relative.

'We came back along the road by the river,' her russet-haired landlady said, 'and it looks as if your boss has got visitors.'

With her foot on the bottom step of the stairs, Gaby looked up. 'Why?'

'There was a flashy white car outside Higher Reaches.'

It was ten o'clock, she thought miserably. It was some refreshment that Erica was having! *She'd* made her departure before lunch and the other woman was still there.

CHAPTER FIVE

THE white car was still there on Sunday and Gaby's spirits continued in a downward spiral. What was happening? she asked herself wretchedly. Was Ethan allowing his ex-fiancée back into his life again? She might look frail but Gaby had sensed that there was purpose and determination inside her and Ethan had soon dispensed with her own company after coming into contact with it again.

One thing was for sure. Time would tell—it always did—and if there *was* a big reconciliation scene taking place inside Higher Reaches the news would soon be around the village, and the staff at Springfield would know about it even sooner.

A case of anorexia nervosa was admitted first thing Monday morning, and when Gaby saw the emaciated young girl in the company of her distraught mother and a social worker her heart went out to her.

Rosemary Beale was seventeen and had reached a state of weight loss that called for the authorities to take over responsibility for her well-being.

'If the girl's weight isn't brought up she will soon be having problems with her internal organs,' the sister on the general ward told Gaby. 'If you observe her closely you'll see that her body is covered in lanugo, a fine, downy covering that is part of the illness.

'She's been admitted to Springfield because there's a shortage of beds at the infirmary and also because her doctor thinks the atmosphere here will be more calming than in a bigger hospital—that she won't feel so conspicuous as she has hysterics if she thinks she's being stared at.

'Our function, which is extremely urgent, is to retrieve her weight loss and a therapist from the psychotherapy unit will attempt to discover what mental hang-ups have brought this state of affairs about.'

'I'm putting her in one of the small side wards to give the kid some privacy, but that will mean closer observation as she won't be on view all the time. That is where you come in, Gaby. You're of a similar age and I want you to keep an eye on her.

'Try to gain her confidence and get her to see what she's doing to herself but, above all, make sure that she eats what she's given and doesn't try to vomit it back. We'll be checking her weight after each meal, but the important thing is that she should *want* to eat as, although she's skin and bone, the girl still thinks that she's fat.'

Rosemary Beale's hair hung in limp brown strands on her bony shoulders. Her skin was white and waxy, her face a gaunt mask full of hollows, and in her eyes fear mingled with defiance.

She had slumped down weakly onto the bed the moment she'd entered the room but once her mother had gone and Gaby approached her in smiling friendliness she said accusingly, 'I suppose you'll be spying on me all the time.'

Gaby laughed, determined to get through to this starved creature whose mind was obsessed with what she saw as the perils of eating.

'Yes, if I have to,' she told her calmly, 'but I know that it's not going to be necessary. We're going to get along just fine because we both want the same thing.'

'What? Not to get fat?'

'No,' she said gently. 'I don't think either of us need worry about that. We both want you to get better and, that being so, I'm sure that I'll be able to trust you. The sooner we get your weight back to somewhere near normal, the sooner you can get back to your friends and your hobbies. Your mother was telling me that you want to be a ballerina.'

'Past tense,' the girl said surlily. 'I've messed it all up. I'm too fat.'

'Have you looked in the mirror recently?' Gaby asked. 'Because if this is what you call fat I wouldn't like to see you when you were thin.'

She'd said it with easy laughter but her young patient, determined not to be won over, said, 'I don't need any pep talks.'

It was clear that winning Rosemary Beale's confidence was going to be no mean feat, and on a more serious note she said, 'If you'd like to get undressed, Rosemary, I'm going to weigh you.'

As Rosemary gave an aggrieved sigh Gaby told her with brisk cheerfulness, 'I'm afraid that we'll be weighing you all the time so you'd better get used to the idea, eh?'

The needle on the scales hovered on five stones and, concealing her horror, Gaby gave her a gentle hug of reassurance.

'Let's make a deal, shall we, Rosemary? Every time you gain a pound we'll mark it off on a chart. When you've put on a stone we'll have a party and if you're here long enough to put on *two* stones we'll have a night on the town, just the two of us, subject to your parents' consent of course.'

There was a faint stirring of interest and Gaby pushed home the advantage. 'Would you like that?'

Rosemary shrugged. 'I suppose so.'

'Good,' Gabby enthused. 'And now it's dinnertime, so let's see how you get on.'

The food put before the young anorexic had been carefully measured. It was very light, to avoid any discomfort to the abused digestive system, but extremely nutritious and as she sat on the edge of the bed and watched Rosemary's half-hearted attempt at eating Gaby's dark eyes were full of compassion for the mixed-up, skeletal figure beside her.

She hadn't seen anything of Ethan and she wondered if he was still entertaining his unexpected house guest. A matter that came under discussion as she stood with Cassandra in the restaurant queue at lunchtime.

'How did the colour scheming work out on Saturday?' the blonde sister-in-charge asked curiously as, having been served, they went to find a table.

Gaby pulled a wry face. 'It didn't.'

'Why was that?'

'When we got to Ethan's place he had a visitor.'

Cassandra's curiosity was increasing. 'Who was it?'

'The woman he used to be engaged to.'

'Really?'

'Yes. She said that she was just passing through but I think she stayed most of the weekend.'

'I see,' Cassandra said slowly.

'I wish I did,' Gaby told her glumly.

'You're in love with our boss, aren't you?' her companion probed.

Her face flamed but she saw no reason to deny it— not to Cassandra, anyway.

'Yes, I am. Do you think I'm stupid?'

'No. I don't. Ethan Lassiter is a very attractive man. If he wasn't so aloof there would be lots of competition but he does rather keep himself to himself and, from what I've heard, it's something to do with this person that you say turned up at his house over the weekend.

'You're a beautiful girl, Gabriella,' she said sincerely. 'I don't see how he could resist you.'

'Oh, he can, all right,' Gaby said grimly. 'Part of the time he thinks I'm positively infantile.'

'And the rest?'

'We have had our moments.'

'Well, there you are. Don't be defeatist. I'd say that you are just what he needs.'

Gaby laughed ruefully. 'Yes, but would *he* agree?'

'I don't know but you're sure to find out sooner or later and—talk of the devil—here he is, fresh from battling with the managers of the Trust.'

It was true. Ethan had just entered the restaurant and was glancing around him with his keen blue gaze. When he saw them he came across and said, 'Mind if I join you both when I've been served?'

'No, of course not,' they chorused, but by the time he appeared with his tray Cassandra was ready for off.

'You'll have to excuse me, Ethan,' she said apologetically, 'but I promised to ring Bevan in the lunch hour. He was making enquiries about a house we're thinking of viewing, as the cottage is a bit cramped for the three of us. It was all right when just Mark and I were there but now we're ready to spread our wings a bit.'

'Sure, go ahead,' he said immediately. 'Hope it's what you're looking for.'

Gaby could feel her heart beating faster. This was their first meeting since the unexpected encounter of Saturday lunch time and she was bursting to know what had been going on, but there was no way that *she* was going to be the one to bring up the subject.

Ethan did it for her, up to a point. 'Enjoy your weekend?' he asked casually as he began his meal.

'No,' she told him truthfully.

'Why not?' he asked, with an annoying lack of surprise.

'I spent Saturday afternoon playing Scrabble instead of juggling with pastel colours.'

'Hmm,' he murmured. 'That was unfortunate—Erica turning up just at that moment. I certainly wasn't expecting her.'

'Yes, I could tell that. What did it turn out to be... a lovers' reunion, or had she come to atone for her sins?' she couldn't help asking.

She was cringing inside, doing the very thing she'd vowed not to...poking and prying about what had gone on when it was none of her business.

However, one thing was for sure, she was getting through to him. At her last question his mouth had tightened and he was observing her guardedly.

'And what sins would those be?' he asked with a tight-lipped intensity that made her feel suddenly nervous but, nervous or not, Gaby couldn't resist the opportunity to pursue the matter.

'I don't know,' she said with assumed casualness. 'One can hardly class colour-blindness as a sin. It's more of a medical problem like Bell's palsy.'

'What on earth are you talking about?' he asked with dangerous calm.

'Well, she has to be colour-blind to have desecrated the inside of your house as she has, and if she persists in driving an open-topped car at this time of the year the lady is asking for Bell's palsy.'

Gaby was aware that although Ethan had asked her to explain what she was rambling on about he wasn't listening. He had put the shutters up against her and disappeared behind them.

Her mood of inquisitive flippancy was evaporating

fast as he started to eat in a mechanical fashion and, where before she hadn't been short of words, now she was tongue-tied.

He looked up suddenly as if her confusion was registering and said in a more normal manner, 'She's gone, anyway...back to the stockbroker belt and the high living that she enjoys so much.'

Relief flowed through Gaby in a comforting tide. So he hadn't changed his mind. Madam Grey Eyes was still out of his life and, unless she took it upon herself to make any more pit-stops in the village, was likely to remain so.

'And so how did the meeting with the managers go?' she asked, as her normal bright beam came from behind the clouds that Erica had cast.

He laughed. 'That was only one question. You're not on form. What's happened to the second one that's always on the heels of the first?'

'Don't push it,' she threatened. 'I can soon think of another.

'Such as?'

Gaby eyed him sombrely. Her head was full of questions but she wasn't sure that they were the kind he would want to be asked like, for instance, was he as attracted to her as she was to him? Didn't he think that people might find it strange that they were always in each other's company? And last, but far from the least, was he indulging in a little light flirtation with a young member of staff because she made it so plain that she was available, or was it genuine passion that had set him on fire the other day in the hospital store-room?

With a quick flip back to sanity, she eyed his empty plate and said, 'Such as...did you enjoy your meal?'

'Yes,' he said briefly, 'and, in reply to the first

question, my meeting with the managers went very well for once. The estimates from the estates department were all under twenty thousand so I can sort out my own funding, which I prefer to do. It's far better than having to go to the finance director, cap in hand.

'It's fortunate that it's merely a matter of change of use. The fabric is there. It's not as if it means a new building and so, with a bit of luck, in the very near future I might see one of my aims accomplished.

'What has been going on this morning in my absence?' he asked, with a change of subject. 'Anything of interest?'

'A teenage girl with anorexia has been admitted and she's in a pretty poor state. The sister on General Ward has asked me to try to create some sort of rapport with her but, weak as she is, Rosemary Beale is also somewhat uncooperative.'

Ethan frowned. 'She wasn't on my list of admissions for today.'

'No,' she agreed. 'Sister said she'd been sent to Springfield mainly through a bed shortage at the infirmary, but it's also supposed to be because it's less traumatic here.'

As if to contradict the statement an ambulance came through the hospital gates, its siren blaring urgently, and as they got to their feet—Gaby to return to the wards and Ethan to his office—it stopped on the forecourt outside the restaurant window.

Almost immediately the doors were flung open and two paramedics lifted out a stretcher on which lay the still figure of a teenage boy.

Gaby felt Ethan tense beside her and when she looked at his face there was consternation on it. 'That's young Mark, Cassandra's boy,' he said in dismay. 'Go and find her, Gabriella, while I see if Bevan is on the premises.'

He was already leaving the restaurant at a run and Gaby made for the office of the sister-in-charge with similar speed, but she was too late. Cassandra had just heard and, white-faced, she was flinging herself round the desk and heading for the corridor.

Fortunately Bevan *had* been in the hospital and, as she watched them trying to take in what had happened, Gaby's heart ached for them.

Mark had been playing rugby, the sport so dear to his heart. A tackle had brought him to the ground and he'd been knocked out for a few seconds.

'It must have been the way he fell,' the agitated sports master who had accompanied him in the ambulance was saying. 'I've seen it happen dozens of times without any cause for alarm.'

'How long has Mark been unconscious?' Bevan asked tightly.

'Since just before the ambulance came,' the man said. 'He went down with a tidy crash and was knocked out for a couple of minutes. When he came to he seemed all right and was all set for carrying on with the game but I made him sit at the touchline. By the time the match was over his speech was slurred and he was very dazed. The next thing we knew he'd slumped over into unconsciousness.'

Bevan Marsland looked at his wife's face and without him needing to speak she said raggedly, 'We have to get Mark to a neurologist, don't we?'

'Yes,' he said bleakly. 'He needs a CT scan. I'm not happy with his reflexes, for one thing. There could be internal bleeding inside the skull, Cassie. It's a freak accident and until we get him to Neurology we won't know what's wrong.'

'Why did you bring him here?' Cassandra asked in anguish of the paramedics. 'He should have been taken straight to the infirmary. They have more facilities there.'

'Yes, we know,' the man agreed, 'but the school where they were playing is just down the road and you do have a casualty unit here.'

Bevan held her close. 'They did what they thought was right in the circumstances, Cassie,' he said gently, and to the paramedic, 'We'll have him back in the ambulance, please, lads, and then as fast as you can to the infirmary.'

As they watched the ambulance drive away with Cassandra and Bevan sitting grim-faced beside the unconscious boy, Ethan said soberly, 'The three of them had so much going for them and now this.'

'Poor kid,' Gaby said softly.

'Yes, and poor Cassandra and Bevan. Cassie brought Mark up on her own as a single parent until Bevan came onto the scene and now he fills the role of stepfather and uncle with all the loving care of a real dad.'

'Mmm,' she murmured with unconscious wistfulness. 'It is to be hoped that they give him some brothers and sisters. Being an only child can be very lonely at times.'

'Don't I know it,' he agreed.

'I've decided that when I get married I'm going to have lots of babies,' Gaby told him. 'How about you?'

She would have loved to suggest that it could be a joint effort if he would stop looking back, but she had no way of knowing how he saw her. Was it as a desirable woman? Or as a colleague who was available for a quick dalliance when the opportunity arose, or did he see her as an irresponsible, pushy young madam, only too aware of her own attractions?

When she looked at him his face had closed up, his eyes were veiled and his mouth unsmiling, as he said, 'I *did h*ave thoughts along those lines but they came to nothing.'

'You mean because of Erica?' she probed carefully.

'Yes.'

'She didn't want children? A lot of trendy people don't these days.'

'It wasn't possible for her to have them,' he explained stiffly.

Gaby's face contorted. This was a new side to him. 'You threw her over because of that?' she exclaimed. 'Poor woman!'

'Poor woman, indeed,' he echoed with the ice still in his voice. 'And now that you've finished questioning me, maybe we can both get back to our separate functions.'

'Sure thing,' she agreed with a lack of warmth that equalled his and, with her young back straight as a ramrod and her head held high, she took herself back to the job on hand with disillusionment as a companion.

He was a tough nut, she thought as the doors of the general ward swung to behind her. He'd given no explanation for his harsh decision but then he had a built-in arrogance about him, hadn't he? That *he* could do no wrong!

She hadn't particularly taken to his ex-fiancée. Erica was too brittle for her liking, but really! If the woman couldn't have children she shouldn't be punished for it, no matter how keen Ethan might be to become a father.

The boot could easily have been on the other foot—

that *he'd* been found to have a low sperm count. Would he have been so high-handed then?

She'd fallen in love with a man who wasn't on the same wavelength when it came to compassion, she thought dismally. Passion...yes. They were in tune there, but lust was no good without liking, and in the long term that was what mattered.

Yet it must have been a strange relationship if that part of it had only become an issue in the last week before the wedding. Surely they would have discussed it long before that? Rejecting her on the eve of the wedding was the cruellest thing a man could do to a woman.

But Rosemary Beale was waiting for her in the small side room and when Gaby looked into her hollow young face she put Ethan and his affairs firmly out of her mind.

Mark Marsland, as he was now known since his mother's marriage to his father's brother, was taken to Theatre for a craniotomy shortly after having the CT scan.

'Extradural haemorrhage,' Nicholas Page, the neurologist at the infirmary, told Cassandra and Bevan with sombre brevity as Mark was being prepared for the operation, 'and even though you're the last two people I should need to explain the procedure to I'm going to, nevertheless. I shall open up the skull, drain the blood clot and clip the ruptured blood vessel in that order.'

Cassandra winced and Bevan's face drained of colour and, observing them, the long, lean, consultant said, 'The burr holes I make will be closed again immediately it's done, and you can take comfort from the fact that we've got Mark here so quickly. I've known folks walking about with this kind of bleed for days, but the success rate is excellent when the patient is operated on promptly.'

Cassandra nodded and went into her husband's outstretched arms as if that were the only place where she could exist with the pain that was inside her.

'What can we do?' Bevan asked him raggedly.

'You can do what relatives of the sick always have to do...wait,' he said briefly, as he strode off in his pristine white coat.

'This guy is good, Cassie,' Bevan whispered against the springing gold of her hair. 'He's young, clever and knows his stuff.'

'I hope so,' she said tearfully. 'I really do hope so!'

Back at Springfield gloom had fallen over the hospital with the news of the serious consequences of Mark's accident and as Gaby prepared to go off duty that evening she met Joan Jarvis coming out of Ethan's office.

Her face was solemn and when she saw the pretty, dark-haired nurse Joan said, 'I've just heard about young Mark. I called in to see Cassie, and Ethan has just been telling me what's happened. I must go to her,' and she bustled off before Gaby could say anything.

The ex-matron manager was heavy with her child. A small, plump woman to begin with, the pregnancy seemed to have doubled her size and as she hurried to her car her breathing was laboured and her legs swollen. Gaby, a few steps behind, wondered if the staff at the antenatal clinic held at Springfield every Friday were aware of her condition. Or maybe Joan Jarvis was under a gynaecologist privately.

Whatever arrangements she'd made, surely a woman who'd previously held a position like she had would have the sense to take care. It was her first child and she *was* in her early forties. It went without saying that Joan would have had the necessary tests to make sure that the baby was healthy but there was her own condition to consider and, from what Gaby had just seen, there could be cause for concern.

A footstep from behind brought Ethan level with her and, remembering her disillusionment of earlier in the day, Gaby gave him a cool nod. He eyed her with equal chilliness and, showing how much he was tuned in to her thoughts, he said, 'You're judging me with regard to something that you know nothing about, Gabriella. I don't remember holding an inquest about your relationship with this Italian fellow but you seem to think *you* have a right to know what goes on in *my* life.'

I *have*! she wanted to cry. Because I love you. Everything about you matters to me, even down to what aftershave you use, whether you sleep in pyjamas or if you like your toast crisp or soggy.

Instead she questioned calmly, 'You're saying that I'm nosy and interfering?'

'No, I'm not,' he replied with equal sang-froid, 'but you are very quick to judge.'

'Let's just say that if *I* were engaged to you I'd be a mite concerned in case I turned out to be flawed in some way...not up to Lassiter standards.'

'I don't consider myself as perfect,' he rapped back, 'but, yes, I do have standards.'

They had reached his car in the parking lot and as he unlocked the door he said, 'Want a lift?'

'No, thanks,' she said with continuing aloofness. 'I'll walk.'

'Suit yourself,' he said drily, and drove off, leaving

her with the knowledge that it had been a disturbing and upsetting day.

The news next morning at Springfield was that Mark had come through the operation safely and was now conscious and coherent. There was a general feeling of relief and thankfulness amongst the staff that one of their own had been spared what might have been a tragic outcome to the situation and Gaby's own lowness of spirit was banished by the good tidings regarding Mark.

She liked Cassandra Marsland. She was efficient, attractive and had been very supportive to her in the months since she'd commenced working at the small community hospital. Gaby would have hated to see tragedy shatter the obvious happiness of the sister-in-charge.

'Good news about Mark, isn't it?' Ethan said when he popped his head round the door of Rosemary's small room. 'He's a lucky lad. Nicholas Page is no mean performer in Theatre. I don't think there's a neurologist to beat him in the whole of the Midlands.'

Yesterday's disenchantment shelved, she gave him her wide, brilliant smile. 'It sure is. It's awful to see the young laid low. I spent quite some time in paediatrics when I was training and, because I adore kids, it wasn't easy to stay detached while caring for a sick child.'

Ethan was eyeing her consideringly and she thought that she'd brought the subject of children up again... not intentionally but she had done so nevertheless and, aware that she was starting to gabble, she went on perversely, 'That is the only complaint I have here... We rarely admit children to our wards.'

'That's because we're not geared up for them,'

Ethan said immediately. 'We haven't the space for a separate children's ward and I'm sure you wouldn't want to see small tots mixed in with the adults.'

'No, of course not!' she exclaimed. 'That would be totally wrong.'

They were holding a sensible, meaningful conversation, so why did she feel that they both had other things on their minds? Gaby knew that *she* had and there was a look in *his* eyes that had her puzzled.

'And how are *you* feeling this morning, Rosemary?' he asked, with a swift change of subject.

'Rotten!' she said ungraciously.

'And why is that?' he asked with a gentle sort of patience that made Gaby envious.

'I'm going to be sick.'

'If you are, it will mean having breakfast all over again,' he told her, 'and I'm sure you wouldn't want that, would you?'

As Rosemary's bony young face crumpled Gaby put her arms around her. Her eyes met Ethan's as she did so and, without him having to speak, she knew that he was thinking that here was another 'poor kid'— the only difference being that Rosemary's troubles were self-inflicted and Mark's were the result of a freak accident.

He sent for her later and when Gaby went into his office, with eyes wide and wary, he said, 'There's no need to look as if I'm going to eat you. I merely wanted to ask if you'd like us to continue from where we left off on Saturday.'

She stared at him. 'You mean colour schemes?'

'Yes. What else?'

What else, indeed? she thought. For an ecstatic moment she'd thought he'd meant carrying on from their passionate encounter in the deserted store-room.

'Yes, I suppose so,' she agreed casually. 'So you didn't decide to keep to the original decor?'

It was Ethan's turn to be surprised. 'Of course not. Why should I?'

'No reason, except I thought that perhaps Erica had taken root.'

His brow darkened. 'I'm not with you, unless... Do you mean to say that you checked up on how long she stayed?'

Gaby knew that it would be useless to lie and in any case she'd never been any good at telling fibs.

'Someone mentioned late on Saturday night that there was a white car outside your house.' She wasn't going to tell him that she'd also done a reccy herself on Sunday.

'And from that observation you deduced that Erica and I were reconciled?'

'Maybe,' she said offhandedly.

'You're a crazy woman! Do you know that? *I* didn't invite her to come here. It was *her* idea...and now she's gone. So what is it to be? *Are* you coming round to talk about the decorating or not?'

She swallowed hard. 'Why are you snapping at me like that if you're supposed to be immune to the charms of old Grey Eyes?'

He got to his feet and beckoned her to him and as she moved slowly forward he said, 'Why do you think?'

Gaby shook her head numbly, and he said with continuing exasperation, 'Don't come the innocent with me, Gabriella. I'm irritated because you obviously think I haven't got a mind of my own; that I don't keep to my decisions.'

'I don't think that at all!' she protested. 'I would imagine that once you've decided something the Rock of Gibraltar would be easier to shift than you!'

'Yes, that's true in most instances,' he said drily, 'but not where *you're* concerned, I'm afraid. That first day in the churchyard I knew you would be trouble and I've vowed to steer clear of you a dozen times since, but each time I do you practise your witchery on me and we end up like this.'

'Like what?' she breathed as he encircled her in his arms.

'You know what,' he said huskily as he reached up and raked his fingers through the thick, dark tail of her hair. Ethan had taken her by surprise with his sudden approach but it took Gaby only seconds to respond, and as they clung together, lips to lips, breast to breast, thigh to thigh, she was riding along the pathway to the galaxies that she'd dreamed of...with this man who had taken her heart into his capable hands.

But what about the way he'd described her? He'd said she was trouble. Hardly a flattering description for someone that he was kissing with a thoroughness that had her spellbound. Maybe Ethan was just using her, she thought painfully. Using her youth and what he saw as her inexperience for some clever game of his own.

The idea had her mind whirling and she tore her lips away from his. 'I'm not into witchcraft, Ethan, and I don't play games with people either,' she cried. 'The way I behave is me, Gaby Dennison. You're always telling me that you see me as trouble. If that is so why don't you stay away from me, instead of summoning me to your office and inviting me round to your house to sort out colour schemes?' And on that angry note she departed.

CHAPTER SIX

IT WAS nearly a week before Gaby saw Ethan again and in every moment, awake or sleeping, he was in her thoughts.

When she'd arrived at Springfield the morning after tearing herself frenziedly out of his arms, she had discovered that he'd gone away for three days to a conference, and when he came back their paths just didn't seem to cross. He was either at a meeting, or always in a different part of the hospital to herself.

The weekend that came at the end of the frustrating week was no different. Short of knocking on his door there was no way she could be sure of seeing him, and if he *was* around the village, once again it wasn't where *she* was. The nearest sighting of him was the tail end of his car turning out of the main street and heading for the motorway to Gloucester.

By the following Monday morning Gaby had decided that he was deliberately avoiding her. There was a sinking feeling inside her that he'd written her off as another bad paragraph in his life. Not a chapter...they hadn't known each other long enough for that!

Perversely, after the long fast, when she arrived at the hospital on Monday morning he was the first person she saw, enjoying a joke with Lucinda Beckman of all people, and immediately Gaby's delight at seeing him again was wiped out with pique.

They were on the corridor outside his office, he looking his usual efficient self in a well-cut grey suit, relaxed and smiling, while the bossy orthopaedic consultant was spreading her brash, over-the-top sexuality around like butter substitute.

'Hi, there,' he said as she stalked past. 'Where have *you* been keeping yourself?'

'In purdah,' she snapped. 'It makes life a lot simpler.'

Dr Beckman's cool dark eyes were looking her over with the same detachment as she would observe an artificial joint, Gaby thought mutinously, forgetting that under normal circumstances she was a great admirer of Lucinda's skill.

As she continued on her way Gaby heard her say laughingly, 'Whatever have you been doing to gorgeous Gaby, Ethan? I've never seen her look so sour before.'

Sour! she thought. That was a good description of the way she felt, as if her blood were charged with acid, but always, to make her feel ashamed of her own problems, there was Rosemary waiting for her.

Her young patient was slowly gaining weight. She still looked gaunt and skinny but most of the food she was being given was staying down. Gaby had found her trying to vomit a couple of times in the first few days but now she seemed reconciled to cooperating, and the two of them were becoming friends.

'I wish I were like you, Gaby,' she'd said one afternoon as the young nurse was bustling around the ward. 'You're so confident and attractive.'

'You'll soon be bonny again,' she'd told her softly, 'if you do as we ask of you, and your confidence will come back as your health improves. Don't forget, when you're over this we're going out you and I, aren't we?'

To her delight Rosemary had come up with a

definite yes and Gaby had felt that maybe they were seeing a light at the end of the tunnel.

While the girl was resting in the early afternoon Gaby's mind went back to the day when Rosemary had voiced her youthful envy and she thought rebelliously that confidence and good looks weren't an asset if the man of one's dreams preferred to be on the touchline one moment and out to score the next.

As if on cue Ethan appeared in the general ward at that moment and, watching him through the doorway of Rosemary's small room, Gaby observed him greet staff and patients alike with a brisk friendliness.

It seemed as if everyone was on easy terms with the hospital manager except herself, she thought frustratedly, as in her case it was a matter of being in his arms one moment and cut down to size the next.

'So? I asked earlier where you'd been hiding yourself,' he said when his tour of the ward brought him to Rosemary's room, 'but I don't recall getting a sensible answer.'

'That would be because I'm not a sensible person,' she told him with sweet guile, 'and I haven't been hiding myself anywhere. Why should I, when there is no reason to?'

'Oh, no? Then who was it who couldn't get out of my arms quickly enough that day in my office?'

'I'm sure I don't know,' she said blandly, 'but it wouldn't have been Dr Beckman or your friend Erica as they both strike me as the lingering type.'

Gaby's flippancy hadn't stopped her colour from rising and as he stared at her stonily after the jibe she capitulated. 'We both know it was me so why pretend, Ethan? I thought I was doing you a favour as you'd made it quite plain that you wanted to steer clear of trouble...and trouble being me...well!'

His dark blue gaze was holding her own. There was irritation in it...and something else that was making her senses swim. 'You must have misunderstood me,' he said quietly. 'There are some kinds of trouble that are worth all the hassle. It's finding the best way to cope with them that's the problem, but I'm not here to discuss the complex workings of your mind, Gabriella.'

Ethan's glance went to the sleeping Rosemary. 'Her mother is coming to see me this afternoon and, though I see from her progress sheets that there is some improvement, I wanted to observe her for myself. The psychotherapist isn't too happy about Rosemary's mental condition. She thinks that the weight-watching and training required for ballet triggered off the anorexia and now it is too deep-seated to expect any permanent cure.'

Gaby's face fell. 'I thought we were doing really well,' she told him. 'I've promised Rosemary a night out, just the two of us, when she reaches a certain weight and she's actually beginning to get keen on the idea.'

His smile was quizzical. 'Well done! Keep it up. I can see that you're using a psychology of your own, but I'm afraid that I'm going to have to move you into Geriatrics for the rest of the day as they're very short staffed on there. In fact, the whole place is running on fewer staff at the moment—with Cassie still off with Mark and Flora Travis dithering as to whether to take early retirement after her heart attack, and holidays among the staff.' He sighed. 'I could go on for ever.'

'But who'll look after Rosemary?' Gaby asked as she eyed the sleeping girl.

Ethan glanced out on to the ward. 'The staff on

here, of course. If the door is left wide open they'll be able to see if our young anorexic gets up to anything that might impede her progress.'

'Does Rosemary know that her mother is coming to see you?' she asked. 'She can be very temperamental sometimes.'

He nodded. 'Yes, I know she can. Her mother is coming to see *her* first and will, no doubt, inform her of our appointment, and now that I've satisfied you that Rosemary will come to no harm in your absence, off you go, eh?'

'Yes, of course,' she said obediently, aware that she had some nerve questioning his judgement but, as always, she had to say her piece and she pointed out, 'I wouldn't exactly say I was satisfied.'

'I see,' he said slowly, with a glint in his eye that she couldn't immediately identify. 'Well, in that case you'll have to remain *unsatisfied*.' And he stepped back to let her pass, waiting for her to depart. As she went Gaby fired her parting shot.

'Being unsatisfied seems to be the norm in my life of late,' she told him, dark eyes wide with protest, and with an attempt at a provocative swish of her sensible plain blue dress she went.

Gaby was attending an elderly lady who had been brought into Springfield in a state of collapse after nursing her husband through a series of leg amputations prior to his death when one of the SRNs from the general ward came in to say, 'Young Rosemary has done a runner, Gaby.'

'What?' she gasped in horror as she gently lowered the patient into a chair beside the bed.

'Her mother had been closeted with Ethan Lassiter for a progress report, but before she went into his office she went to see her daughter and when she'd gone Rosemary was in a terrible state.'

'Why, for heaven's sake?' she asked distractedly. 'And how did she manage to get through the outer ward without being seen? Surely someone was with her while she was in that state?'

Her heart was thumping. How many times in her first few days at Springfield had the girl said that she wished she were dead? But they'd put all that behind them...hadn't they?

The other woman swallowed uncomfortably. 'One of the nurses had been with her but she'd been called away and we don't know how she managed to get out. Ethan is going spare about it. There have been red faces all round. He's got everyone available searching the hospital and the grounds, but so far no joy.'

'And what about her mother?'

'Blaming herself for upsetting her.'

'And so she should,' Gaby said grimly. 'What did she say to cause Rosemary to do this?'

'Seems she told her she was getting married again. Her husband died a year ago and Rosemary was gutted when they lost him.'

Gaby groaned. 'What tact! What sensitivity! Hasn't the kid enough to cope with at the moment without being informed that her father is going to be replaced after such a short time? I can't believe that...'

She stopped suddenly, transfixed by the thought that had just occurred to her. 'I saw a flash of something bright red a few minutes ago amongst the trees that lead down to the river. Rosemary has a dressing-gown that colour!'

Her hand flew out to grip the other nurse's arm. 'Fill in for me here, will you? I'm going to look.' And before the other woman could answer she'd gone, her long legs taking her out of the hospital and through the grounds at the fastest pace she'd ever done.

It was there again, a flash of bright scarlet this time in a heap on the river bank, but there was no sign of Rosemary—until Gaby looked down into the river's deep water and saw her floating in it like a limp white doll.

As she jumped in voices sounded from nearby and there was the noise of bracken snapping beneath running feet but they were sounds that didn't register. Nothing in Gaby's life before had ever mattered so much as getting Rosemary out of the river.

She could swim as well as she could run and though there was stark fear in her it wasn't for herself. As she broke the surface, pulling the girl with her, Ethan's head bobbed up beside her out of the water and he said coolly, 'Hold on, my brave, beautiful girl. Between us we'll soon have her out.'

Gaby nodded grimly. It was a moment for action, not words. At any other time his description of her would have been music to her ears, but all that she could hear now was the pounding of the water as they struck out against it with Rosemary's limp form between them.

It could only have been a matter of seconds before they reached the steep bank but to Gaby it seemed an eternity and, as willing hands reached down to pull them out, all she could think of was that Rosemary musn't die.

There was no shortage of volunteers to start resuscitation and as she stood shivering beside the unconscious girl, watching the frantic efforts to revive her, it was the sweetest sound on earth when Rosemary gave a weak splutter and then started to retch.

By this time Gaby's uniform was clinging to her

like a second skin and Ethan ordered brusquely, 'Get inside, Gaby, and strip off those wet clothes and, when you've done so, have a long hot soak to take the chill out of you. Rosemary's going to make it and the moment we get her wrapped in dry blankets one of the doctors will check her lungs for any water retention or other problems.'

She nodded meekly and went to do his bidding on legs that were far from steady. She would have liked to point out that he was just as soaked as she was but if she started fussing over *his* well-being in front of the rest of the search party there would be some raised eyebrows and, though *she* didn't care a damn, it went without saying that *he* wouldn't be too chuffed.

By the time Gaby had scrubbed herself clean and found a spare uniform from somewhere Rosemary was back in bed, looking absolutely ghastly but, according to the sister on duty, none the worse for her self-inflicted immersion.

'Why did you do a silly thing like that?' Gaby asked her gently as she perched on the side of the bed.

'I was fed up because what I've known all along had just been proved right,' she said weakly.

'And what was that?'

'That my mum couldn't have loved my dad.'

'What makes you think that?'

'Because she's going to marry his best friend... Tommy Bradshaw.'

'Did you tell her how you felt?'

Rosemary shook her head, 'No. There was no point. She's only interested in herself and, in any case, if she didn't know before...she will now!'

'It was a rather drastic way of voicing your opinion, wasn't it? If you've any doubts as to whether she loves you it's a pity you didn't see the state she was in when we brought you out of the river.'

'That would be guilt.'

'Some of it perhaps, yes. It would have been wiser if she'd waited until you were stronger before telling you her plans but she says she thought you'd be pleased.'

'Well, she thought wrong. I don't want a stepfather!' Her pale face crumpled. 'I want my dad!'

'I'm sure that must be how your mum feels too,' Gaby told her softly, 'but he's gone, Rosemary. Your dad is dead and if he could speak to you I'm sure that he would tell you both to get on with your lives; that he doesn't mind about your mum and Tommy and he wants *you* to feel that way too.'

The girl's face was clearing and her eyes were less hostile as she said, 'Do you think so?'

'I'm sure,' Gaby told her firmly, 'and now I want you to do something for me.'

'What is it?' she asked warily.

'Have a good long sleep, and when you awake forget all about what has happened today. OK?'

'Yes,' Rosemay agreed, her eyelids already drooping, 'and thanks for saving me, Gaby.' She gave a drowsy chuckle. 'Tomorrow I'll tell you how I got past the guards.'

Gaby laughed back. 'Yes, you do that, but only on one condition.'

'What's that?'

'That you promise never, ever to do it again.'

'I promise,' she said as her voice slurred into sleep.

Gaby looked down on her sadly. Rosemary's reckless act of momentary depression could only make matters worse for her, physically and mentally, and yet good might come out of it.

If the true extent of her grief over the loss of her father hadn't shown up during psychotherapy sessions its contribution to her mental state might not have been noted, as Rosemary had never discussed her father's death with her. In fact, the first Gaby had known of it was only a few minutes ago, so reticient had the girl been about it. That being so, it could be equally to blame, along with the obsession over weight loss with regard to her ballet aspirations.

Whatever the outcome of it all, a long, tortuous road lay ahead of Rosemary and Gaby felt like weeping over the disastrous incident. Yet there was no one she could blame. Ethan had a hospital to run and he'd sent her where he thought she was needed most.

The fact that it had left an anorexic young girl at risk was something that he couldn't have foreseen. He wasn't to know that the girl's mother, with the best of intentions, was going to knock the last prop from under her daughter's feet. Neither could he have expected that the vigilance of the staff on General ward would be any less keen than her own.

'When they told me that one of my nurses had gone into the river after Rosemary Beale, I knew it would be you,' his voice said suddenly from behind.

As she swung round to face him Gaby wondered how long he'd been there. His hair lay damply against his head, his face had lost its healthy colour and the saturated shirt and trousers had been replaced with grey trousers and a blue lambswool sweater.

At the sight of him Gaby was consumed with an overwhelming longing to throw herself into his arms and cry her heart out, but there was a questioning expression on his face, as if he was waiting to hear her verdict on what he'd just said, and, being who she was, she didn't disappoint him.

'Why were you so sure it was me?' she asked quietly.

'Because I knew you would be frantic when you heard Rosemary was missing...and because you don't know the meaning of fear.'

'Right on the first count... Wrong on the second,' she informed him. 'I *was* frantic, yes. Because even though I'd obeyed orders I was uneasy about her. As to my never being frightened, you're wrong there. *You* scare me to death and I was petrified I wouldn't be able to get her out of the water in time. Believe me, it was a very welcome sight when I saw you surface beside me.'

'It was the least I could do,' he said drily. 'Bad enough to lose a patient but a member of staff as well! I could see myself telling the managers of the Trust that there'd been a double drowning.'

Gaby glared at him. 'Thanks a bunch! I must have misheard you out there in the river. I thought I heard you describe me as brave and beautiful! The last thing I'd want to do is mess up your records and to think I could have gone to that great ward in the sky without having told you that I'd like my ashes scattered on the Bay of Naples.'

Ethan's face had darkened, and as he moved towards her he said angrily, 'You're treating what happened out there in the river as some big joke. Well, I don't think it's funny. I didn't at the time...and I don't now!'

'Neither do I,' she gulped as tears flooded her throat, 'but sometimes, when the hurt is too great, the only thing to do is laugh.' And, as his face softened and he reached out for her, she swept past him and didn't slacken her pace until she reached the staff-room.

* * *

Cassandra came back on duty the following day and when she heard what had happened she sought Gaby out.

'That was a brave thing you did yesterday,' she said immediately. 'I have the greatest respect for our local waterway. I very nearly drowned in it myself.'

'When was that?' Gaby asked in surprise.

'It was before you came here. We'd had torrential rain that caused the river to overflow and we had to evacuate the hospital. I was the last to go and got swept away in it.'

'That sounds horrendous!' she breathed.

Cassandra grimaced. 'It was, but good did come out of it. Bevan and I had both been trying to pretend that we weren't crazy about each other but when he found me all wet and weary...but safe...the barriers came down and we revealed to each other our true feelings.'

'That is how it seems to be with me and Ethan,' Gaby said glumly. 'I can't make him out. When all the trauma of Rosemary's frightening behaviour had calmed down he referred to the fact that she and I could have been drowned as if it only concerned him from the hospital's point of view.'

Cassandra smiled. 'Wouldn't you say that was typically male? He'd probably been going insane at the thought of losing you, but once you were safe he decided to play it down so that you wouldn't get too cocky.'

'Oh, he thinks I'm that all right,' she admitted ruefully. 'But enough of my affairs. How is Mark?'

'Coming along fine, thanks. He had a very lucky escape.' She shuddered at the memory. 'Bevan and I wouldn't like to go through that again and neither would he. When she heard what had happened his grandma flew over from Brisbane to be with us and

I've left him in her care today. They haven't known each other all that long but they get on a treat. And now, what about Rosemary Beale? She's put herself back light years with yesterday's crazy behaviour.'

'There was a reason for it,' Gaby told her sombrely. 'Her mother had just given her some devastating news without having the gumption to take note of the child's reaction, and when she'd gone to keep her appointment with Ethan Rosemary fled the hospital, a desperate little skeleton making a cry for help. The mother wants her head examining!'

'It's clear that you feel very strongly about it,' Cassandra commented.

'Yes, I do,' Gaby admitted, 'but who am I to take up the cudgels on her behalf...a mere staff nurse?'

The sister-in-charge laughed. 'Don't put yourself down. You are a force to be reckoned with, as I'm sure our boss will agree.'

'That's not how he sees me,' she protested. 'To him I'm trouble.'

'I'd have thought they both meant the same thing,' Cassandra said as she went on her way.

That night Gaby gave in to persuasion and let Simon Baird take her for a drink. He'd asked her out several times since his mother's dinner party but she'd always refused. However, when he rang this time she agreed to go to the Goose with him.

One reason was because all her fellow boarders at Cleeve House were elsewhere. Hank, the American, had gone to a different part of England to drink in the atmosphere, the schoolteacher had gone home to his parents for half-term and Noah was attending his mother-in-law's funeral, which left Gaby high and dry as far as company was concerned.

But the main reason for her agreeing to spend the evening with Simon was her lack of progress in getting to know Ethan better. She felt thwarted because every time they met there was some sort of friction between them and she didn't want that, even though she was usually the cause of it.

When they walked into the cosy country pub, paradoxically he was the first person she saw and immediately the evening took on a new meaning.

He was chatting amicably to Mike Drew, one of the GPs who practised at Springfield, and his clingy girlfriend, and when Simon saw him he said irritably, 'He *would* have to be here!'

Gaby shrugged. 'Ethan *does* live in the village,' she pointed out. 'He has as much right to be in here as you or I, and why get rattled about it?'

'I'm rattled because I sense something between the two of you,' he grumbled.

'Rubbish!' she hissed as she raised her hand in casual salute to the man they were discussing. Mike Drew had also become aware of their presence and he gave her a shy smile.

Gaby liked the mild-mannered GP. Mike mightn't be endowed with a sparkling personality but he was an excellent doctor who, in spite of his rather possessive companion, was obviously well smitten with Cassandra.

You've no chance there, Mike, she'd thought a few times. Our sister-in-charge has eyes for no one but her very attractive new husband and who can blame her?

She'd reasoned that maybe that was why she felt this empathy with him. They were both yearning for someone out of reach. In his case permanently so. Not so in her own, though. There was plenty she could do to make Ethan want *her* as much as she desired *him*.

After all, he'd already proved that he wasn't immune to her. He probably wasn't immune to chickenpox either, and, that being so, he wasn't going to go rubbing up against somebody with watery blisters.

You're being defeatist, Nurse Dennison, she told herself while a disgruntled Simon was at the bar ordering their drinks. Ethan Lassiter might be top dog at Springfield but you're just as useful a cog in the wheel as he is, and when you're both off duty...well!

You're in love with him, yet you do nothing about it and it's time you did. And, not being the sort to sleep on a decision, Gaby met the thoughtful blue gaze that was encompassing her from across the room with an inviting smile.

It must have worked because, while the expression was still on her face, Ethan came across and said casually, 'Why don't you both join us? Joan and her husband are coming in later. Cassie and Bevan too, as long as Mark is feeling OK, and our favourite orthopaedic wizard, Lucinda Beckman, said she might drop by.'

Gaby's face straightened. So much for charm! A cosy evening in the pub had been arranged by all the people she liked...and loved...but the juniors weren't invited, which she supposed was fair enough except that wasn't how she saw herself in relation to Ethan. She'd found out about it by accident and now she was being asked to join them as an afterthought!

'No, thanks,' she said with brief politeness as her escort loomed up with a glass in each hand. 'I'm not all that keen on invitations that come as an afterthought...and...in any case... Simon and I want to be alone.'

She knew that she was being petty and stupid, and when she saw Simon's face light up she groaned inwardly. Some tangled web she was weaving! But she'd got the bit between her teeth now and the devil at her elbow.

If Ethan had planned a cosy evening with the hierarchy of the local health service she was going to see to it that his attention was diverted...in *her* direction.

Unfortunately she wasn't dressed for seduction, in a white ribbed sweater and a black skirt, but she had the long legs and the mane of glossy dark hair that hung in tendrils around a face like a golden rose, and whether Ethan Latimer was geared up for 'trouble' or not...it was on its way to him.

From the moment of deciding that, Gaby was at her most fascinating—eyes dancing, full red lips smiling all the time, every movement of her body provocative—and if she wasn't getting through to Ethan she was certainly having an effect on Simon.

And because she admitted shamefully to herself that she wasn't being fair to him she endured his arm possessively around her shoulders, his lips nuzzling her neck, and tried to ignore the message that went with it.

'Mum and Dad are staying at my gran's tonight,' he said towards the end of the evening. 'We could sleep together at our place.'

'I don't sleep around, Simon,' she told him in a milder voice than the one she would have used if she hadn't been feeling so guilty. She was acutely aware that if he had the hots for her, the same couldn't be said for the man that she'd tried to entice. His eyes were like cold blue glass in a face that looked as if it had been hewn from granite.

'The next thing you'll be telling me is that you're a...' His voice faltered over the word.

'Virgin?' she prompted softly. 'As in freak? Yes, I am, strange as it may seem.'

'Yes, it *does* seem strange,' he said angrily, 'considering the way you've been giving me the come-on all evening!'

'It wasn't directed at you,' she said placatingly. 'If it seemed that it was it's because I never did have a good sense of direction.'

'Really? Well, there's nothing wrong with mine and it's pointing me in the direction of home. Goodnight!'

As Simon slammed out of the room Ethan got to his feet and strolled across to where Gaby was sitting in complete mortification.

'And what was all that about?' he asked with steely calm.

'I think he was disappointed that I'm still a virgin,' she said, saying the first thing that came into her head.

'And why did that subject come up?'

'Why do you think?'

'He wanted you to sleep with him?'

'Yes.'

'I'm not surprised.'

'Meaning?'

'Meaning that it would be hard for any man to resist you in the mood you've been in tonight.'

'Except you?'

'What have *I* got to do with it, Gabriella?' he asked with dangerous calm. 'You came here with young Baird and were at great pains to make it clear that you wanted to be alone with him.'

'Yes, I did, didn't I?' she said flatly as she got to her feet. 'I wonder when I'm going to get something right?' And, reaching for her jacket from a nearby coatstand, she opened the door and went out into the winter night.

CHAPTER SEVEN

ETHAN caught up with her on the pavement outside Cleeve House and, taking her arm, he swung her round to face him.

'What is it with you, Gabriella?' he said irritably. 'I asked you to join my friends and me but you refused, which was fair enough if that was how you felt, yet you couldn't leave it at that, could you? *You* didn't want my company but you made sure *I* didn't get the chance to enjoy anybody else's. You were determined that I would be so aware of you that I couldn't concentrate on anyone or anything.'

So her efforts hadn't all been in vain. She almost smiled but knew that it wasn't the right moment. 'You seem as if you don't know your own mind half the time,' he went on. 'It's no wonder young Simon went off in a paddy.'

'*Young* Simon takes too much upon himself,' she said coolly. 'He was suggesting that we sleep together and we hadn't even kissed! When *I* get around to sleeping with a man he will have courted me first... and married me. That is, providing he doesn't want me to take a fertility test before we tie the knot. It could be a bit off-putting having to prove one is suitable for breeding purposes.'

If Ethan had been tetchy before she had unleashed fury in him now and, gripping her wrists, he pulled her up against him and glared into her eyes.

'How dare you bring up my past in such a manner?' he said furiously. 'You are spouting forth about something that you know nothing of. You're just a little too eager to say your piece, Gabriella. I don't regard your sex in that light at all so don't be so quick to form opinions!'

Gaby's face had lost its colour. He was right, of course, like he always was. His affairs were no concern of hers. She had hit out at him in her misery and insecurity and unleashed a frightening tide of anger, and now she was desperate to put matters right.

He had dropped her wrists and was turning to go but she pulled him back. 'I'm sorry, Ethan,' she breathed. 'I do deserve to be told off. It's only when I'm with *you* that I behave like this. I'm sure you must have had a very good reason for doing what you did to Erica.'

His face was still dark and unsmiling as he told her, 'You don't really think that so why pretend?'

There was entreaty in her eyes. 'It's what I want to think.'

She wanted him to tell her the truth but why should he? As he'd already pointed out, his past was not her concern. Yet she thought longingly that his future could be—it could be the most important thing in her life if it was bound up with hers.

'When you asked us to join you and the others in the Goose tonight I refused because I'd only gone there with Simon for lack of better company,' she told him. 'I would have much rather been with you but the moment he clapped eyes on you Simon started moaning and he would have been even worse if we'd joined forces.'

'But why, for God's sake? What have I ever done to *him*?'

'He thinks there is something between us,' she told him softly.

'Really? And what do *you* think?'

'I think there could be if you would let it.'

'So you don't see yourself as the stumbling block?' he asked with a gleam of amusement in his eye.

She swallowed. 'You know perfectly well how I feel, Ethan, but you prefer to keep me at arm's length, and all because another woman didn't come up to scratch.'

Gaby knew she was treading on dangerous ground again and it was foolish as she really didn't want to push them any further apart.

'There are a few reasons I could give for keeping you at arm's length,' he said imperturbably, 'and they are nothing to do with my past. The first one is that you're very young. You haven't had time to meet other men or see what the world is made of.'

Gaby put her hand over his lips. 'I met Giorgio and that was an enlightening experience, and I'd had other dates before he came into my life. I don't feel young when I'm with you, Ethan. The ache inside me is as old as time itself.' But he was gently removing her fingers from his mouth and he went on as if she hadn't spoken.

'The second is that I prefer to be the hunter not the hunted, and the third reason why I try to keep you on the fringe of my life is because of this,' and as his lips found the soft hollow of her throat he murmured, 'this insanity that makes me want to kiss every inch of you...that makes my loins ache for you...when all the time I know that I should leave you alone, let you enjoy your young life.'

He cupped her face in his hands and kissed her lips just once in a gesture of farewell, and then he turned to go, and she could find no words to stop him.

* * *

As winter wrapped itself more closely around the Cotswolds the promise of Christmas glowed like a bright lantern. Last year Gaby had spent it in Sorrento. She'd gone there in late November when the SOS had come and they'd celebrated it together, she and her *nonna*, with brave laughter and treasured gifts, grateful for the mild weather of the Sorrentine peninsula.

This time when it came it would be very different. She would be free to celebrate the season in whatever way she chose. Yet *was* she free? Last year she'd been tied to the sick-room. This time she was just as tied but the shackles were invisible to all but herself. They were bonds of her own making and she wasn't sure whether she could cope with spending Christmas on the edge of Ethan's life, relegated to his circle of acquaintances.

As the days went by, with a cool sort of friendliness their only contact, it became harder to believe that the times when he'd held her in his arms with such raw passion had actually happened.

Not being prone to inactivity, Gaby was inevitably restless and frustrated at the lack of progress in their relationship and she had to keep reminding herself that she'd been warned off. Ethan Lassiter was his own man and he'd made it clear that if there was to be any pursuit it would be done by him...not her. But so far he'd shown no signs of wanting to get to know her better and there wasn't a lot that she could do about it.

But there were to be other happenings before the Christmas bells pealed out. In the thirtieth week of her pregnancy Joan Jarvis was diagnosed as having pre-eclampsia and she was admitted to the maternity unit at the infirmary to be kept under observation.

When Gaby enquired about her, a worried Cassandra told her, 'Joan has shown rapid weight gain recently. Her blood pressure is up and they've found protein in her urine. The odds aren't really in her favour at the moment as she's a primigravida, and over thirty-five into the bargain. She's coping with the problem in her usual calm capable manner but Bill is totally distraught at the thought of anything happening to Joan or the baby.'

'Pre-eclampsia usually clears up of its own accord after the birth, doesn't it?' Gaby said.

'Yes,' was the reply. 'The real danger is if it should become eclampsia. It certainly would be panic stations then!'

Two other memorable happenings that were happy rather than sad were the small party on the ward when Rosemary put on her first stone and, as her weight started to creep up to the second and she was shortly to be discharged, the night out that Gaby had promised her.

Ethan had given his permission for her to take the young girl to a disco at a club in the nearest town, but only on the condition that he took them and brought them back.

'I'm quite capable of taking care of both of us!' Gaby had protested when she heard his stipulations.

'That may be,' he'd said implacably. 'But while Rosemary is a patient at Springfield, and hopefully she won't be for much longer, she is under my care. I'm responsible for her and there is no way that I'm taking any chances. You haven't forgotten that we almost lost her once.'

'I'm hardly likely to forget that, am I?' she'd said frostily. 'I still have nightmares about it.'

'So do I,' he'd told her grimly, 'and not just because of her.'

'Oh, so you didn't really mean it when you referred

to what might have happened as messing up your statistics.'

For a moment it had almost been as before, when the vital spark was apt to flare between them at the slightest thing.

'What do *you* think?' he'd asked softly and then, as if to put her back on the leash, 'I couldn't live without my tormentor.'

'Nor I without mine!' she'd flung back, but, having said his piece, he was already departing, straight-backed, inexorable, and infuriatingly out of reach.

Rosemary's mother had bought her a new outfit for the disco and when she was ready Ethan was going to pick her up at the hospital and then call round at Cleeve House for Gaby.

When she saw her young patient in a gold miniskirt and a tight black top that showed off her hard-won weight gain it was hard to believe that this was the thin waif who had come to them all those weeks ago.

For herself she'd chosen to wear green flared silk trousers and a flame-coloured blouse and, because she couldn't resist seeing any impact she might make on Ethan, she went out into the chilly night carrying her jacket.

'You look very Italian tonight,' he said in a low voice when he got out to open the car door for her.

'The Sorrentine side of me must have overcome the Brum,' she said with a low laugh. 'My perfume is of lemon groves instead of carbon tetrachloride.'

His eyes were warm and Gaby felt her blood start to race, but Rosemary was watching them from inside the car and so she slipped into the seat beside her and they were off.

When Ethan deposited them on the pavement outside the club Gaby asked, 'Is it to be like Cinderella? We have to leave on the stroke of midnight?'

'No, it isn't,' he said immediately. 'You have to leave on the stroke of eleven o'clock. Rosemary is still a patient at Springfield and this is her first time out for quite a while. I don't want it to be too much for her.'

'Why don't you join us?' she asked, willing him not to go away, but she should have known better. If Ethan thought *her* an infant at twenty-one he wasn't likely to fancy dancing the night away with a seventeen-year-old.

'Two's company, three's a crowd,' he said calmly, 'and I've arranged to meet someone in the Grand Hotel bar. I'll see you both on the dot of eleven o'clock.'

Gaby scowled at his departing back. So he'd slotted them into his other engagements, had he? And who was he meeting in the Grand Hotel? The thought of Ethan ensconced with some beautiful woman amongst the understated elegance of the town's finest hotel had taken the edge off the disco already.

But not for her young charge. Rosemary's face was one huge smile, her eyes bright, her feet moving, and, whatever her own thoughts, Gaby couldn't help but be glad to witness the change in the girl.

In the middle of the evening a touch on her shoulder made her turn to discover Simon Baird behind her and she stifled a groan, but it wasn't herself he was after.

'Aren't you going to introduce me to your friend?' he said, and, after a moments hesitation, she obliged. When Simon led Rosemary onto the dance floor Gaby thought that for once he had come in useful. It would do wonders for the girl's confidence to have a young male around on her first night out of hospital.

Gaby was determined that they would be ready and

waiting when Ethan came back for them, but when she looked around the club at ten minutes to eleven Rosemary was nowhere to be seen.

Her heart began to thud. If he arrived to find the girl missing her own reputation would be in shreds. She'd been quick enough to brag that she was capable of looking after her, and if Rosemary was going to prove her wrong she would want to curl up and die.

She searched around frantically but Rosemary was not to be seen—and neither was Simon Baird. Gaby clenched her hands with angry frustration. She should have known better than let him monopolise Rosemary. The guy was trouble as far as she was concerned. Whenever he appeared on the scene things went wrong.

Ethan's face was set in stone when he got out of the car and saw her standing alone on the pavement. 'Where's Rosemary?' he asked immediately.

'I don't know,' she told him miserably. 'Simon came and foisted himself on us and he's been dancing with her all night.'

'You mean to say that you've let her go off with that...whippersnapper without taking note of where they were going...what they were doing? I don't believe it!'

'All right!' she flared back, trying to conceal her dejection. 'It takes two to botch things up. Rosemary knew as well as I did that she was out on licence.'

'God!' he exploded. 'You make it sound as if she's been let out of prison.'

'If the cap fits! You're the head warder, aren't you?' She was being aggressive and knew it was unfair, as she was to blame, but it was the only way to stop herself from bursting into tears and howling like a banshee. All her caring, her efficiency, had come to nothing and she was presenting a picture of gross carelessness.

'There she is!' he cried suddenly, pointing to a taxi that was pulling away from the curb. 'And that young devil is with her. Blast his hide!'

Gaby's legs had gone weak and she wondered if that was how it felt when a person fainted with relief but Ethan was grabbing her arm and pulling her into the car and as they tailed the taxi he said grimly, 'She's not going to escape a second time.'

If there was anything to commend the whole distressing episode it was that Rosemary had asked to be taken back to Springfield. At least she hadn't let Simon take her somewhere else and, remembering his request to her that she should sleep with him on very short acquaintance, it was a relief that the other girl hadn't succumbed to any such persuasion.

The moment the taxi stopped Ethan was out of his car and challenging them and, with a sudden feeling of unutterable weariness, Gaby got out of the passenger side and began to walk away.

She didn't want to hear the whys and wherefores of what had happened or to endure Ethan's scorn again. She'd done her best and, between her boss and her patient, her spirit had been crushed.

When the car pulled up behind her as she trudged through the dark night she knew that it was Ethan but she carried on and it was only when he stopped and ran to catch her up that she turned.

'Are you insane, or what?' he bellowed. 'Walking the roads alone at this time of night?'

She didn't answer and made to walk on but he swung her round and when he saw that her face was wet with tears his eyes widened.

'What is it?' he asked quietly. 'What's wrong? Rosemary is back in the ward safe and sound.'

She sniffled. 'Is she?' she said dully. 'Good. The next time she goes anywhere send someone else with her.'

'The next time she goes anywhere it will be home,' he said decisively, 'and I think that is where you need to be.'

'I haven't got a home,' she told him with forlorn dignity. 'There are a couple of rooms available to me. One at Cleeve House and another at my father's place in Birmingham but they're not home to me, merely stops along the way.'

He took her hand and held it against his cheek. 'Stops along the way to where?'

'You tell me. I'm one of the country's floating population.'

'Perhaps I should do something about that, then?'

Even in her gloom Gaby couldn't resist saying, 'What do you mean? Take me for a child bride? Or as a nanny when Lucinda and yourself start a family?'

'Lucinda? What has she to do with anything?'

'I can smell her perfume on you and I'd expect the Grand Hotel to be her scene. She must feel as if she's slumming when she comes to the Goose.'

'I've spent the evening with one of the managers of the Trust, trying to twist his arm for some extra funding,' he said patiently as if she were a troublesome child. 'If you smell perfume on me it's from the cloakroom girl. Apart from you, she's the only woman I've spoken to all evening.'

'I see,' she said indifferently.

'I wonder if you do,' he said, his voice deepening. 'I wonder if you can see that I'm not indifferent to you; that I have to take a hold on myself otherwise we would never be out of each other's arms. I'm employed in health care but there is no prescription for what ails me. It's an Anglo-Italian virus that's got into my bloodstream and I'm hoping that a cure might soon be found.'

'Why do you want to be cured?' she asked with the indifference still inside her.

He had his answer ready as he traced her lips with a gentle finger. 'Because I feel as if it's not the only thing wrong with me that might be catching. Such as disillusionment, or an enforced sort of caution.'

'I'm too fed up for listening to big words,' she said, leaning against the car like a broken reed.

'Perhaps you're too fed up for this too,' he said softly as his mouth caressed hers, gently at first and then with increasing ardour, but he knew, didn't he, that she would never be too fed up for that?

But as she kissed him back Gaby knew that it didn't alter anything. Ethan was being nice to her because she was upset. It didn't change the fact that he thought her incompetent and over-confident, and when he drew away from her, his eyes questioning her lack of response, she said sadly, 'I don't think there will ever be a right time for us. Everything I do is a disaster, and none bigger than imagining I could ever come up to *your* required standards.'

As the taxi that had taken Rosemary and Simon back to Springfield cruised past she lifted a limp hand and flagged it down and as Ethan stared at her in disbelief, she got in and, after giving the man directions, she slumped down dejectedly on to the seat in the back.

'I'm sorry about last night,' Rosemary said uncomfortably when Gaby went into her room the next morning.

'Yes, and so you should be,' she told her with a wry smile. 'You got me into a lot of trouble with my boss. Where did you both get to, for heaven's sake?'

'We went out through the back door of the club to get some air and I lost track of the time. I knew that we had to leave at eleven o'clock but Simon kept saying there was no rush, and then it was too late and I couldn't face you so we got a taxi.'

'If I know Simon Baird he would have taken you out the back door for more than a breath of air,' Gaby said laconically. 'Am I right?'

Rosemary's face went bright red. 'Yes, but it was only a quick cuddle.'

'That's all right, then.' And she gave the squirming teenager a quick pat on the shoulder. 'You're entitled to a bit of fun after all you've been through, but please, next time, don't get me involved, eh?'

The girl smiled with visible relief and to Gaby's amazement she said, 'I've been thinking about what I'm going to do when I get out of here and I want to take up nursing.'

'You do?'

'Yes. I've had a chance to see hospital life at first hand for quite a while and, though it's been from the position of patient, it hasn't put me off a career in health care.'

'Good for you,' Gaby proclaimed. 'Nursing is hard work but it has its rewards. Take you, for instance. You're fit and well again. You've got some flesh on your bones and I just know that you're going to stay that way.'

'Can we keep in touch after I go home?' Rosemary asked.

'Of course we can,' Gaby assured her, 'and how about making a pact?'

'What about?'

'That whichever one of us gets married first they ask the other to be their bridesmaid.'

Rosemary's eyes glowed and she clapped her hands. 'Yes! I'd love that. But will Mr Lassister approve?'

Gaby stared at her. 'Ethan! What has he got to do with it?'

'Well, he's in love with you, isn't he? I can tell by the way he looks at you.'

'Then you're more observant than I am,' she told the girl pensively. 'Most of the time he treats me like an irritating child.'

'Not from where I'm sitting,' Rosemary teased, and Gaby gave her a playful push.

'I can see that your romantic five minutes with Simon Baird is making you see everyone else's relationships through rose-coloured glasses. You know that his mother is in charge of physiotherapy here, I take it?'

'Yes, he told me, and he's asked me for a date when I'm discharged.'

'Really,' she murmured. 'Well, nobody could say that he isn't a fast worker.'

Before she could expound any further on Simon Baird's virtues, or lack of them, Ethan's voice said from the doorway, 'My office, please, Gabriella.'

'I presume that Rosemary has told you what happened last night,' he said with crisp formality as he motioned for her to take a seat opposite.

'Yes, she has.'

'Extremely thoughtless of her to go wandering off as she did and young Baird is even more to blame.'

'Simon wasn't aware of the circumstances of her presence at the club,' she told him in reluctant defence of the youth. 'It was only when she started panicking about it being gone eleven o'clock that he found out that she'd been allowed out of hospital.'

'Nevertheless, the two of them put you in a very difficult position and I saw to it that they were made fully aware of the fact.'

She smiled. 'I've forgiven them both.'

He frowned. 'A night's sleep has obviously banished your distress. One can't beat the resilience of the young.'

'I didn't ask to be born later than you,' she said indignantly, 'just as *you* had no say in the timing of when you were conceived, and if you think that I'm deliberately bringing up the subject of having children again, well, I'm not!'

'I didn't think you were,' he told her with weary patience, 'but your curiosity is still there, isn't it?'

'No, of course not,' she fibbed. 'Why should it be?'

'I'm sure I don't know.' He was pulling a pile of paperwork towards him across the desk and when he looked up he said, 'And I really haven't the time to start making conjectures.'

As she turned to go he called her back. 'Let me take you to lunch to make up for last night's fiasco, eh?'

She bounced back immediately at the unexpected invitation and when he said, 'How about the Grand Hotel at one o'clock?' her eyes danced with anticipation.

'How about it!' she replied. 'It will give me the chance to sniff the cloak-room girl's perfume.'

'Can I have an extra half-hour for my lunch?' she asked the sister on General when she got back to the ward. 'I'll make it up at the end of the day.'

'I don't see why not,' was the reply. 'There's always room for an extra pair of hands when we're changing shifts in the evening.' She glanced around the ward where every bed was occupied. 'We've got a full house today, and nearly all of them Dr Beckman's joint replacements. These days the demand for new knees almost equals that for new hips. When the ambulance rolled up while you were away they had 'em packed in like sardines.'

Gaby was eyeing a woman who was walking about without difficulty but with evidence that she'd had surgery to her chin, and she said curiously, 'Surely *she* isn't one of Lucinda's patients?'

'She is, indeed. That lady had little or no gum at the bottom of her mouth, which meant that when she'd had her teeth removed for health reasons a denture just wouldn't stay in place and so the orthopaedic team have taken a piece of bone from her hip and transplanted it into her bottom jaw.'

'Very impressive.'

'Very impressive indeed,' the sister agreed.

Fortunately Gaby had spare clothes in her locker and so was saved from having to lunch with Ethan in her uniform. In the cream jacket and dark green dress that she kept there for emergencies she would feel more at ease, and was grateful for the opportunity of giving him the chance to see her in something other than the blue cotton dress.

Also, most conveniently, it was only a ten-minute bus ride into the town, and when Ethan arrived she was seated at a low table in the bar area waiting for him.

He wasn't looking too happy and Gaby's heart sank. What had she done wrong now? As he seated himself beside her he said with an edge to his voice, 'When I asked you out to lunch I wasn't intending you making your own way here. I *do* have a car.'

'You don't!' she said in mock surprise.

'Stop fooling, Gabriella,' he growled. 'The last thing I intended was that you should have to use public transport! If one of the SRNS hadn't seen you at the bus stop I would have been searching the hospital for you.'

She was smiling, relieved that for once she was in the clear. 'You said Grand Hotel, one o'clock,' she pointed out with sweet reason. 'There was no mention of bringing me here and as I thought that you mightn't want to be seen leaving Springfield with me I got the bus.'

'Well, of course I didn't mention it,' he said in exasperation. 'I imagined that you would take it for granted that I would bring you here. What sort of a moron do you think I am?'

'I think you're a lot of things, Ethan,' she said with unaccustomed gravity, 'but never that, and if we keep harping on about our lack of communication, which of course is not unusual, the lunch hour will be gone and I'm starving.'

He smiled then, and as Gaby feasted her eyes on the strong planes of his face beneath the thick corn-coloured hair he said, 'Let's get you fed then. There is usually an excellent buffet on offer in the Bristol Suite.'

As they got to their feet he took her arm and his touch was delight, his nearness joy, and the knowledge that for a short time she had him to herself was paradise.

'I wondered what you would wear,' he said as they helped themselves from an array of appetising dishes. 'Uniforms are a necessary thing but they can be a nuisance sometimes when one wants to socialise. But obviously you are prepared for all eventualities,' and she thought with a rush of pleasure that the warmth in his eyes was approval and if there was anything she sought, it was that.

With her smile as bright as the lighted chandelier above them and her dark eyes glowing, she told him, 'You're right about the uniform. I get tired of being dressed in blue. There are so many other colours that I adore.'

'Such as flame-red, gold, turquoise, yellow?'

'How did you guess?'

'Because they're vibrant shades. Full of warmth and colour like yourself.'

'Is that how you really see me?' she breathed as a waiter showed them to a table.

'You know very well it is,' he said with a matter-of-factness that brought her back down to earth, but she wasn't to be put off.

'Then why don't you do something about it,' she said recklessly, 'instead of keeping me on ice?'

'Ice!' he hooted. 'I'd like to see anybody try to do that. You're too much of a sizzler. And in any case I thought we'd gone into all that.'

'*You* might have, but *I* haven't!'

'Eat your food,' he said, like a father to a chattering child, 'and if we've got ten minutes to spare we'll call at the infirmary to see Joan Jarvis.'

The mention of his predecessor's difficult pregnancy was enough to make Gaby push her own problems to the back of her mind and she asked, 'How is she?'

His face was grave. 'Responding to medication, but she'll be in there until the baby is born, I think. She and Bill are ecstatic at becoming parents so late in life but everything has a price, and I just hope that Joan and the baby come through it all right.'

'Thanks for the lunch,' she told him as they got up to go. 'It was a delightful change from the hospital's corrugated cottage pie.'

'It was my pleasure.'

'Was it really?' she challenged.

He sighed. 'Don't be dense, Gabriella, of course it was.'

'It wasn't an exercise in staff relations, then?'

'Yes, I suppose it was, up to a point. My asking you out was first of all in way of an apology for the way you were messed about last night. There aren't many of my staff who would give up an evening, after working all day, to take part in patient rehabilitation and then get told off at the end of it for something that wasn't their fault.'

'And that's it, then? You didn't bring me here because you wanted to be with me?'

'What would you do if I said yes?'

'This,' she said immediately, and her arms went around his neck, her soft lips claimed his and, to her delight, it was there again, that fusing of the senses that had to mean that he loved her as much as she loved him—but she'd forgotten one thing.

'I prefer to be the hunter. . .not the hunted,' he'd told her once, and as he put her from him she knew that he was remembering his own words, but he didn't voice the fact. He merely said, 'If we don't get a move on we won't have time to see Joan,' and as Gaby nodded she was deciding that there was too much misery involved in loving Ethan Lassiter and she wasn't going to give him another chance to repulse her.

CHAPTER EIGHT

'IT's rest period between half-one and half-two,' the sister on the maternity unit at the infirmary told them when they asked to see Joan, 'so make it brief, please.'

They exchanged smiles. As far as she was concerned they were just visitors, and both Gaby and Ethan found it amusing to be on the other side of the fence.

Joan, when they found her, was calm, resigned to the enforced rest. . .and huge, and when Gaby had presented flowers that she'd bought from a stall at the hospital gates and Ethan a couple of new crime paperbacks she told them that it was on the cards that they might induce the baby.

'Obviously the obstetrician is going to hang on as long as he can to give the baby a better chance,' she said flatly, 'but they can't envisage me going full term.'

'How far are you?' Gaby asked.

'Thirty-two weeks,' she said, 'and I'd dearly like to be a bit further on before they induce. One problem is that my blood pressure keeps rocketing but I'm being monitored all the time for that and other problems connected with pre-eclampsia so I can't complain, can I?' she said with a wry smile.

'How is Bill coping?' Ethan asked, and Joan managed a laugh.

'He says there isn't all this trouble when a cow drops its calf but, truthfully, he's worried sick, which doesn't make me feel any better.'

They were both silent on the way back to

Springfield, occupied with their own thoughts, and because they'd been in an atmosphere connected with childbirth Gaby's were with the woman that Ethan had discarded because she couldn't give him children.

There was something strange about it, as most couples didn't give the matter a great deal of thought until the desire for a family came to the fore and if there were difficulties *then* was the time for sorting out who was fertile, and who wasn't, in the partnership.

As she glanced at his firm jawline he turned his head and smiled at her but she didn't smile back. She wanted to justify what he'd done but she didn't know how because he refused to tell her the circumstances.

Any other man would have done so to clear himself in her eyes if he'd had just cause but not Ethan Lassiter. Whatever she didn't like about him she could lump, as far as he was concerned.

When she saw Cassandra later in the afternoon Gaby told her that they'd been to see Joan.

'Together!' the sister-in-charge exclaimed.

She smiled. 'Yes, Ethan took me out to lunch and we called at the infirmary afterwards.'

'Really?'

'It was by way of an apology, that's all,' she said quickly. 'I kept my promise and took Rosemary out last night but the village Romeo, Simon Baird, came on the scene and spirited her away and guess who got told off for it?'

'You?'

'Mmm. However, when Ethan heard the true circumstances he forgave me and took me out to lunch.'

'I see,' Cassandra said unconvincingly. 'A nice gesture.'

'It would have been if it was because he was

desperate for my company,' she said folornly, 'but I doubt that was the case.'

'I'm not so sure about that,' her companion said. 'Whatever you might think about his motives, you're the only female that he's given a second glance since he came here and there are some who will be envying you at this very moment.'

'They don't need to,' Gaby told her flatly. 'If ever there was a relationship that isn't going anywhere, it's mine with Ethan Lassiter.'

The workmen from the estates department came the next day to start on the flat conversion, much to Ethan's satisfaction, and as the hospital swung into its smooth daily routine the noise of hammers and saws in the background were a reminder of the progress in health care that its manager sought.

Gaby was helping Mike Drew in Casualty and the first person they saw was a youth who was having difficulty swallowing, due to very swollen neck glands.

'How is it that you didn't go to your GP with this?' Mike asked as he examined the lad.

'Haven't got one,' he croaked. 'We only moved here yesterday from Weston Super Mare, and one of the new neighbours said it was better to come here as there's always a long wait at the infirmary.'

Mike gave a dry smile. 'It sounds as if your informant hasn't heard of the Patients' Charter but, as you're here, let's get you sorted out, eh?'

'I saw my own doctor before we moved because this throat bug was making me feel really rotten, but the stuff he's given me seems to be making it worse. I've got a rash now and I can hardly swallow at all.'

'What did he prescribe?' Mike asked immediately

as Gaby looked on with interest. They'd both already noted that the lad had a temperature and that his tonsils were enlarged and very sore, along with swollen lymph glands in the neck, groin and armpits.

'Ampicillin.'

'Ah! So that is why you're feeling worse, laddie,' he told him. 'You're being treated for a bacterial infection when, in fact, it's not. I'm almost certain that you've got glandular fever.'

'What's that, Doc?' he asked in alarm.

'An acute viral infection that brings with it a very sore throat and swollen glands. It can cause mild liver damage too, and you do appear to be slightly jaundiced.'

There was panic in the lad's voice. 'So what are you going to do?'

'Take a blood smear and then send you home...to bed. When I get the result I'll be round to see you and if it is what I think it will be a case of complete rest for a few weeks until it leaves your system.'

When he'd gone Mike said, 'The disease spreads quickly amongst young teenagers...often through kissing.'

Gaby grimaced. 'Ugh! What a gruesome thought for a kid to catch something so unpleasant from a delightful thing like a kiss.'

That same afternoon Lucinda Beckman came to visit her patients. Gaby was checking the dressing of a man that the orthopaedic consultant had operated on for claw-hand when she appeared, and as she approached the bed Lucinda asked casually, 'Ethan around?'

'I would imagine so but I don't know exactly where he is,' Gaby said quietly.

She nodded. 'I'll find him when I'm ready.'

I'm sure you will, Gaby thought grimly, and hoped

that it would be her patients that she wanted to discuss.

'You understand what I've done, don't you, Jack?' she was saying to the patient. 'I've cut a tendon in your hand to release your fingers from the clenched position.'

'Yeah,' he grunted, 'not a pretty thought but somethin' had to be done, hadn't it, Doctor?'

'It certainly had. That's what happens when the ulnar nerve gets damaged and in your case it was so severe that it was no use trying splints.'

'So I'll soon be able to go back to work?' he said.

'It all depends on what you do,' she said cautiously.

'I'm a grave digger, amongst other things.'

'Ah! Well. I think it may be a week or two before you're handling a shovel again but you'll get there—the operation and physiotherapy should do the trick.'

There was gratitude in the man's eyes. 'Thanks, Doctor. I have every confidence in you.'

Lucinda gave him her patronising smile. 'And so you should have!'

When she'd gone the patient, a burly man in his fifties, rolled his eyes and said, 'A good doctor, but would you say a bit queenly?'

Gaby laughed. 'Dr Beckman is the best for your sort of problem. She's brilliant. You're in good hands with her.'

He grinned back. 'That's all I want...good hands, so as I can lift a shovel...and a pint tankard.'

Rosemary was discharged the following day and when her mother came to pick her up there were farewells all round for their much healthier looking patient. When it came to Gaby's turn she gave the girl a hug and reminded her that they were going to keep in touch. 'And don't let Simon Baird talk you into doing anything you shouldn't,' she admonished gently.

'I won't,' Rosemary promised laughingly as she snuggled into the warm winter coat that her mother had brought.

When she'd gone Gaby looked around the small room that had been home to the young anorexic over the past weeks and she sighed. Hopefully, Rosemary would never again slip into a state of mind that made her see food as the enemy but there was no gaurantee.

Another deep trauma like losing her dad, or her unfulfilled ambitions to join the ballet, could spark it off and she prayed that during the months to come Rosemary would find the strength to keep any such neurosis at bay.

Apart from anything else, self-imposed malnutrition could be responsible for the start of osteoporosis, a condition that would only manifest itself later in the girl's life, and its effects could be devastating.

Ethan and Cassandra came in at that moment to interrupt her gloomy reverie, and as he looked around the empty room Ethan said philosophically, 'It won't be empty for long. If it were we'd be out of a job,' and then as he saw her downcast face, 'Cheer up, Nurse Dennsion. It's going to be one of those days when everything goes right.'

'The Friends of Springfield have just delivered three hundred new books for the hospital library and, wait for it, all small rooms such as this are to be made *en suite* and vanity units installed beside each bed in the two main wards.'

'We must be doing something right,' Cassandra said laughingly and Gaby nodded in smiling agreement. It was good to see the man she loved on top of the world but what a pity that the job was the only thing that really turned him on.

'As you know, it was our reaccreditation earlier this

year and we came through with flying colours,' the blonde sister-in-charge told him. 'Maybe we're reaping the rewards.'

'That, and a lot of entreaty on my part,' he said drily, 'but, whatever the reason, as long as we're given the chance to improve our standard of care that is all that matters.' And he went on his way, a man on top of his job but in his private life an enigma.

As Christmas drew nearer so did Gaby's birthday, and on a chilly day in the second week in December she became twenty-two years old.

In spite of the occasion she was without her usual bounce for a number of reasons. One of them was the fact that Noah, her favourite amongst the lodgers at Cleeve House, had gone home. The motorway extension was finished and his services were no longer required.

Gaby was happy for him that he would be back working nearer home but sad to see him go, as his robust good nature had helped her through moments of loneliness and it had also been there to share the crazy times when she'd been on top of the world.

He hadn't been aware that most of her fluctuating moods were connected with her boss but he'd been prone to remind her that some guy was going to be very lucky one day and that he wished that *he* was thirty years younger.

His teasing had made her wonder if Ethan ever wished that *he* were younger so that there would be less age difference between them, but she had a feeling that perhaps the gap was just an excuse to stay clear of entanglements.

Another reason that was making her feel less than festive on her special day was the fact that there'd been nothing in the post from her father and Jessica. They were all the family she had but it looked as if her birthday wasn't as pressing a matter to them as the clothes they cleaned.

There would be no celebrating at work either as she hadn't told anyone it was her birthday, and as the morning progressed her gloom increased.

She would go to the cinema tonight, she decided, and take in a meal afterwards, but there wasn't a film on that she wanted to see and the thought of eating alone was depressing.

It was while she was debating what to do that she espied Ethan deep in conversation with the builders and when he saw her he called across, 'Hang on a minute, will you, Nurse?'

Gaby dredged up a smile when he came over, telling herself that at least she'd seen him on her birthday as he wasn't always around due to meetings and other duties elsewhere. But today he was here, not gift-wrapped but his presence a gift in itself.

To her surprise, he said casually, 'We never did get around to sorting out those colour schemes, did we?'

'Er...no,' she agreed.

'I was wondering if you'd like to come round straight from work tonight and I'll rustle up a sandwich or something?'

This was more like it, she thought as her heart lifted. It was beginning to feel like her birthday after all. 'Yes, I'll do that...and thanks.'

He lifted a surprised eyebrow. 'Don't thank *me*, Gabriella. *You're* the one who is doing the favour, and this time, just to make sure that we *are* communicating, I will take you to my house in my car. Yes?'

'Yes.' She glowed, restraining the urge to tell him that she would be prepared to travel in the corporation dust cart if he would be there at the end of the journey.

Gaby went home in the lunch hour to collect something to wear for the evening ahead. Ethan had already seen her in the clothes she kept at work and, unable to resist the chance to impress him, she chose a dress of soft turquoise wool with a black beaded waistcoat and high-heeled black shoes to replace the comfortable flatties that she wore on the wards.

A makeshift meal and a session poring over colour charts were a far cry from a birthday celebration but it was the nearest that she was going to get to it and she didn't mind because she would be with Ethan. Obviously *he* didn't know that the day was any different from the rest of the week, and she was prepared to leave it at that.

When he collected her at the end of the day his face quirked into an amused smile. 'You're looking very swish for an evening of scrambled eggs and satin finishes,' he remarked.

Gaby's colour rose and she said defensively, 'What did you expect? We're only supposed to be choosing the paint...not putting it on.' And not wanting to miss the opportunity of offering her services, she added 'When the actual transformation takes place I will be resplendent in white overalls and a decorator's cap.'

They were walking towards the hospital car park and she gave him a quick sideways glance. 'I hope you didn't tell your friend Erica that I said it was like a bordello.'

His face was void of expression as he answered, 'No, I didn't. Our relationship ending as it did, I felt that she mightn't see the funny side of it.'

As he unlocked the car she said curiously, 'I don't see a connection between infertility and prostitution.'

'Good,' he told her decisively, 'because you're not

meant to and, please, Gabriella, don't ruin the evening before it's begun with questions and erratic judgements.'

Her smile was contrite. 'I'm sorry, Ethan. You've invited me to your lovely house and *nothing* is going to spoil it.' And if you knew that it's the only nice thing that's happened to me today you would understand why, she thought wistfully.

When he opened the door and ushered her into the house she sniffed appreciatively. 'That doesn't smell much like scrambled eggs,' she commented.

'They must be giving the hens a new type of corn, then,' he replied as he waited to take her coat and, as she eyed him dubiously, 'All right, I'll come clean. I popped back in the lunch hour and stuck a casserole in the oven.'

There was a warm feeling around her heart to know that he'd been prepared to take so much trouble for her, of all people, and, dark eyes huge in her beautiful face, Gaby told him, 'You're full of surprises. I never know what you're going to come up with next.'

'I'd have thought that applied to *you* more than me. You are the unknown quantity around here, Gabriella. One moment I think I understand you perfectly...and the next I'm floundering.'

'Floundering!' she hooted. 'In all the months we've known each other I have never once seen you flummoxed. You appear to have nerves of steel and a heart to match.'

Her eyes widened and she clapped a hand over her mouth. 'Sorry! I'm doing it again...passing judgement...and arguing.'

Ethan was opening the door of the dining-room and he called over his shoulder, 'Yes, you are! Maybe a surprise will strike you dumb.'

'A surprise?' she echoed. 'What sort of a...?' Her voice trailed away as her eyes took in the scene. The room was lit with a rosy glow that came from the soft light of lamps and the flames of a log fire crackling in the fireplace.

In the centre a round table was set for two, with scarlet candles waiting to be lit and crystal wine glasses waiting to be filled. Beside one of the places was a small gift-wrapped box and as her eyes went to it Ethan said softly, 'Open it, Gabriella.'

She was rooted to the spot, like someone in a trance, and when he repeated, 'Open it,' she moved slowly towards the table, her face in shadow.

Her fingers were trembling as she lifted the lid and when she saw a bracelet of fine gold, interlaced with glowing stones, and his voice said softly from across the room, 'Happy Birthday, Gabriella,' instead of expressing delight, her face crumpled and she bent her head and wept.

'What is it?' he asked as he took her in his arms. 'Don't you like it?'

That made her really howl. 'Of course I do,' she sobbed. 'It's lovely. I'm overcome, that's all, because you've remembered my birthday.

'I thought nobody cared. I haven't heard a word from my dad, which is not unusual, and I suppose if he *had* remembered he would have sent me something like a couple of dry-cleaning vouchers.

'My *nonna* never forgot, but she's gone for ever, and I wasn't going to tell the staff at Springfield in case they thought I was after presents or a party and, then, you...you of all people...have done this...for *me*. How did you know it was my birthday?'

'Simple, my dear Watson,' he said calmly. 'Have

you ever heard of hospital records? They include each person's date of birth.'

Gaby blew her nose and wiped her eyes, aware that she was still in his arms and wanting to stay that way, but after planting a kiss on her forehead he released her and said gravely, 'If madam would be seated she can sample the house wine while I go to check on the meal.' And with a flourish he pulled out a chair.

The casserole was delicious and, commenting on it, she said wryly, 'Why is it that everything you do turns out brilliantly, while my efforts are usually catastrophic?'

He shook his head. 'Don't believe it. This is my speciality, inasmuch as it's the only thing I can cook. It's where my culinary skills end. We're having ice cream for dessert, and the soup we had for starters was out of a tin.'

It wouldn't have mattered to her if the starters had been washing-up water and the sweet a dry crust, so enchanted was she that he had taken the trouble to look up her date of birth and, having done so, acted upon it. Ethan *had* to care about her. He had to feel the same as she did or he would never have planned this lovely surprise but, being who she was, Gaby had to hear him say so.

As the reflection from the fire glowed in her dark eyes and turned her olive skin to fine amber she said softly, 'Why did you do this for me, Ethan?' She looked down at her wrist. 'The beautiful bracelet and the meal?'

He didn't answer immediately, but now, supremely confidemt that he *must* love her, she was prepared to wait. His face was in shadow, however, and so she wasn't ready for what was to come.

'I did it because I don't like to see you lonely and

neglected. Like myself, you're short on family. As to the gift—' his voice had roughened with an emotion she couldn't define but there was nothing emotional about the way he was completing the sentence '—it is a token of my esteem for a dedicated, hard-working young nurse.'

There was all the hurt in the world in her eyes as she said quietly, 'I see,' and, getting to her feet, she said in the same muted tones, 'May I use your bathroom?'

He was watching her gravely. 'Yes, of course. It's at the top of the stairs.'

Gaby nodded and left the room but instead of going upwards she moved outwards and, slipping the front door off its catch, she ran out into the night, sobbing out her misery as she went.

It had all been done out of pity because he was sorry for her, she told herself, not because he wanted her company or because he loved her as much as she loved him. Was the man blind? No, of course he wasn't. Ethan knew how she felt about him but he *did* like to keep turning the knife.

In her headlong flight she avoided the road and pointed herself towards the river bank, desperate to be out of the streetlights, and when she heard the pounding waters nearby she crouched on a fallen tree trunk and cried until she'd no tears left.

Some birthday it had turned out to be after all, she thought desolately as a chill wind nipped her bare arms but its iciness was nothing compared to the frozen state of her heart.

A twig snapped nearby but she didn't look up and she turned away when Ethan's voice said raggedly from out of the surrounding darkness, 'Gabriella! There you are! Have you gone insane. . .dashing out of the house like that? You're going to get your death of cold out here with no coat on.'

'Go away. Leave me alone,' she said dully, and his concern turned to anger.

'Don't be so utterly stupid. What's that going to achieve? I'm aware that you don't like comments about your youth but if ever I saw infantile behaviour this is it! If you won't came back into the house of your own accord I will take you inside forcibly. So what's it to be?'

'You wouldn't dare!' she challenged.

There was a look in his eyes that made her heart beat faster but before she'd had time to work out what it meant he bent suddenly and, placing his arm behind her knees, lifted her up high and slung her over his shoulder.

Gaby kicked out and squirmed furiously, but to no avail. He carried her as easily as he would have done the child that he'd likened her to.

When they got to the house he marched in without speaking and slammed the door to behind him with his foot. Then with her still in his grip he stood her in front of him and said gratingly, 'What was all that about? One moment we were enjoying a pleasant evening and the next you were hot-footing it out of here as if the devil himself were after you.'

She gazed up at him with a challenge in her dark eyes. Ethan knew how she felt about him and tonight, with just the two of them wrapped in the magic of the firelit room, she'd been sure that he returned her feelings, but he'd warned her off again.

He'd told her why he'd made the meal and bought the gift and it hadn't been because he was as enchanted with her as she was with him. It had been merely a friendly gesture and she hadn't been able to cope with his explanation.

Gaby swallowed hard. 'I ran off because, after making my birthday come to life, you'd just spoiled it by making it clear that your feelings for me consist merely of pity and appreciation of the way I do my job.

'I don't want either of those things from you, Ethan. Certainly not pity, and complimenting me on the way I'm performing at Springfield is gratifying up to a point but it is no different than what you would say to any member of staff.'

She was still in his arms and in that second they tightened around her. 'I'm not immune to your charms, Gabriella—far from it, as you're well aware,' he said raggedly, 'but one of us has to hang onto our sanity.

'However, as I seem to have disappointed you in some way, perhaps I'd better make amends.' And he bent his head to hers.

As his mouth explored hers Ethan began to caress the soft mounds of her breasts and when they sprang into hardness he bent to stroke her thighs.

It was then that Gaby came out of her trance. This was mockery. Ethan was going to make love to her to teach her a lesson. It was his way of saying that if that was all she wanted she could have it, but it wasn't, was it? She wanted his love and respect, as well as his desire, and she was so confused that she didn't know what was on offer, if anything.

It was torture to move out of his arms and agony to push his hands away from her aching thighs, but she did it. As she stood before him and heard his harsh breathing Gaby knew that in a matter of seconds they would have been committed irrevocably to their desire and, even though she loved him desperately and wanted Ethan to be the one to take away her virginity, she couldn't bear it to be like this, with no tenderness between them.

This time she left his house in a civilised manner, aware that not a word had passed his lips since he'd promised her passion and been repulsed as they'd moved towards ultimate fulfilment.

When she got in the car there was still silence between them and it wasn't until Cleeve House loomed up in the darkness that she broke into it to say quietly, 'Thank you for...a...er...memorable evening, Ethan. I won't ever forget it,' and, leaving him to make what he would of that, she opened the car door and walked quickly up the path.

Gaby undressed in a trance-like state. She could still feel the heat of his touch on her skin and she thought that if she hadn't broken away from him when she had her life would have been changed for ever in one way, yet not in another because he still wasn't perpared to tell her that he loved her and there was only one conclusion to be drawn from that...he didn't.

As she drew on her nightgown she froze with dismay. The bracelet had gone! Her wrist was bare. She'd lost his gift only minutes after receiving it. How could she face him in the morning?

In fact, how would she face him about a few things? The bracelet was only one of them. There was the way she'd fled into the night while a guest in his house, unable to accept his bland explanation of why she was there.

And lastly, but most important of all, how would she be able to face him with the memory of their passionate escalation into love-making that had held her spellbound—until the humiliating reason for it had brought her out of her coma.

* * *

It certainly wasn't one of the best night's sleep she'd had. Dawn was touching the sky with rosy light before she dropped off, and before she knew it the alarm was bringing her back to wakefulness and the day ahead.

Her first task before she commenced her duties was to tell Ethan that she'd lost the bracelet. Under other circumstances she would have kept well out of his way after last night, but Gaby knew that she wouldn't rest until she'd confessed its loss and so the moment she got to the hospital she pointed herself in the direction of his office.

He was already behind his desk, looking less than his usual immaculate self, but his voice had its normal brisk tone as he said, 'Ah! Nurse!'

She flinched at the impersonal greeting, but then, what had she expected him to say? Hello, darling?

'I have something for you,' he went on.

Gaby immediately forgot the strained atmosphere and smiled her relief. 'You've found it!'

He frowned. 'I'm not with you. Found what?'

Her face dropped. 'The bracelet. I lost it some time during the evening.'

'I see. Well, I'm afraid I haven't seen anything of it.' There was irony in his eyes. 'It wasn't with you long.'

She hung her head. Whatever else she might think about last night's episode, nothing could alter the thought and generosity that had gone into his gift and she was utterly mortified to have lost it. She'd pushed her way through trees and shrubs down by the riverside in her distress. Maybe it had got caught up in a branch.

It seemed that Ethan was having the same thought as he said evenly, 'I'll have a look down by the river at lunchtime. No point in waiting until tonight as it will be too dark. But, to get back to what I was saying,

I have something for you. It was amongst the morning mail,' and picking up an envelope off the desk he handed it to her.

Her father's handwriting was on the outside of it and her heart lifted. It looked as if he'd remembered after all. Better late than never.

'From your father?' he asked casually.

'Mmm. I think so.'

She found herself dissolving into laughter. There was a card inside and two ten-pound vouchers for dry cleaning at any of the shops in the chain that employed her father.

She waved them in the air so that Ethan could see them and then, as the laughter threatened to turn to tears, she fled.

In the early afternoon Gaby and the sister on the general ward were doing the rounds with the drugs trolley when Ethan appeared.

'I'd like a word with Nurse Dennison when you've finished, Sister,' he said.

The older woman smiled. 'That's what they all say, Mr Lassiter.'

He looked at her blankly. 'Who?'

'All the men who like to talk to a pretty girl...and a nice one at that.'

'Really?' he said offhandedly.

When he'd gone Gaby said protestingly, 'Why did you say that, Sister? He'll be thinking I'm the hospital flirt.'

'Just teasing,' she explained laughingly. 'We've been trying to get him married off ever since he arrived but until you came he wasn't interested.'

'And now you think he is?'

'You tell me.'

'Ethan Lassiter isn't looking for a wife,' Gaby told her firmly.

'Because of his broken engagement?'

'Possibly, or it might be because he's lost interest in that sort of commitment.'

'He'd make some child a good father,' the sister said. 'I've watched him with any children that have come to Springfield for whatever reason and it's clear that he adores kids.'

'More than the average man, would you say?' Gaby asked carefully.

'Yes, I'd say that.'

'So a marriage without them would be more painful to him than most men?' she questioned, aware that she was trying to find justfication for his past actions.

'I would expect so,' the other woman said, puzzled by her persistence.

When Gaby went to his office for the second time that day Ethan was standing by the window deep in thought and when he swung round to face her in answer to his summons to enter he was holding the bracelet in his hand.

'It *was* caught on the branch of a tree,' he said levelly as he held it out for her to take.

Gaby held it carefully in the palm of her hand and looked down on it. The stones in it were all the colours she loved...the colours that he'd likened to her personality...and, ashamed of her behaviour of the previous evening, she said hesitantly, 'I'm sorry about the way I ran off last night. It was rude and ungracious of me, especially after you'd gone to so much trouble for one of your *staff*.'

She couldn't resist putting emphasis on the last word because the hurt was still inside her, but she'd told herself a dozen times during the night that she ought to be adult enough to accept that Ethan could please himself who he fell in love with...and it didn't *have* to be her.

'Let's just forget it, shall we?' he said steadily. 'Maybe I could have handled it better.'

'Maybe we both could,' she told him with characteristic generosity, and as she went back to the wards with the bracelet once more back on her wrist Gaby was telling herself that at least she had a token of his respect, if nothing else.

CHAPTER NINE

HAVING no plans for Christmas, Gaby had offered to work so that one of the nurses with a family might have the opportunity to be with her children but Cassandra had told her firmly, 'The rotas are already made out, Gaby, and you are off over Christmas. But you needn't worry, we've got you down for New Year and that is usually the busiest time, especially in Casualty.'

'I don't mind working both,' she'd insisted, with the thought of being the only boarder left at Cleeve House over the festive season, but the sister-in-charge had been quite inflexible.

'No. You're looking tired and peaky at the moment. The break will do you good. You've got five days off—make the most of them.'

Gaby had turned away listlessly. She'd just had a birthday that had been a mixture of highs and very lows and wasn't looking forward to the next special date on the calendar one bit.

Cassandra was right. She did feel jaded but it wasn't from overwork or oversocialising—far from it. Her lack of zest came from within, and she had to keep telling herself that she must take care that it didn't brush off onto the patients. They would have enough to contend with by just being in hospital at Christmas, let alone their various ailments.

The porters had erected a huge Christmas tree in the entrance and in each of the wards there were swags of fresh greenery on the window-sills and masses of balloons, glittering baubles and coloured lights in every conceivable place.

Amongst it all she laughed and joked, teased and comforted, but it was with a heavy heart, and when a young paramedic waltzed her around the ward where the old folks were and ended up kissing her soundly beneath the mistletoe to enthusiastic applause she forced herself to kiss him back with equal fervour.

It was only when he released her with a laughing, 'Oops! I'll be getting you the sack!' she realised that they'd had an extended audience. Ethan had been standing just inside the doorway watching them with a grim smile, and as she eyed him warily he turned on his heel and went.

So much for that, she thought as she straightened her cap and sank down onto a chair while she got her breath back. Trust the man in her life to appear when she was making an exhibition of herself. But then he was used to her infantile behaviour, wasn't he? He probably thought that as *he* wasn't prepared to fall into her arms she was out to find somebody who was.

James Harrison was eighty-five years old and had been brought in the previous day suffering from hypothermia. His home help had found him in a distressed state and phoned for an ambulance.

His breathing had been slow and shallow, his movements confused and apathetic, and when they'd sounded his heart the beat had been very faint.

The woman had told them in shrill distress, 'Ever since they put the VAT on the gas bills he's been afraid to have his heating on. The poor old fellow has only his pension and a bit of supplementary and he's frightened that he won't be able to pay his way.

The elderly just can't cope with what's going on these days.'

Gaby had nodded in sombre agreement. The old man had probably fought for his country and been a decent citizen all his life and now he was afraid, not of his nation's enemies but of poverty—in one of the most enlightened countries in the world.

They had covered the top of his head because the most heat loss came from there, and he was being warmed gradually beneath layers of heat-reflecting material and given warm liquids to drink.

His rectal temperature had been taken on arrival and would be taken every half-hour until his body warmth, breathing and heart rate improved.

Hopefully he would make a good recovery, but what if it should happen again? Ethan had been in touch with Social Services and someone was due to see him later that day, but the staff felt that the old man would need to be in a less confused condition for any progress to be made with regard to his future well-being.

'We'll be keeping him in over Christmas, won't we?' she asked anxiously of Ethan as they exchanged polite greetings at the man's bedside.

'If we have a bed available, yes,' he answered briefly. 'If not, I'll make sure that he is found somewhere warm and cheerful to stay for the time being.'

'And after that?'

He sighed. 'I don't know. Basically it's our job to get the poor old fellow back on his feet again and then Social Services should take it from there.' He looked down at James's snow-white hair and beard and said with a hint of a smile, 'If we'd been a children's hospital he would have made an excellent Father Christmas once he'd recovered but, having said that, if we'd been a paediatric unit old James wouldn't have been here in the first place.'

Gaby had closed her eyes. She'd just had a vision of the two of them with a small blonde girl and a dark-eyed boy, opening presents on Christmas morning in Higher Reaches, with Ethan dressed as Santa and she glowing and content in the warmth of his love.

But when she opened them the main participant of the scene was already moving away, his mind on other things than what a dewy-eyed young nurse might be imagining.

It was tradition for the hospital to have a staff party the week before Christmas, and this time it was to be held at the Grand Hotel.

As was usual with that sort of occasion, it had been one of the main topics of conversation amongst the staff for weeks and as the time drew near Gaby was undecided whether to go.

She felt that an evening spent watching Ethan with Lucinda Beckman or any other female he might attract would be more than she could stand. Yet it would be even worse if he decided to spend it with *her* as she would know that it was an act, a formality, because she was young and alone—a veritable Cinderella.

The decision was taken out of her hands by Cassandra, who said, 'Bevan and I have invited a few people around for drinks after the staff party. Will you join us?'

She'd hesitated and the sister-in-charge had said coaxingly, 'Do say you'll come, Gaby. It will be Mark's first adult event, for one thing, and a celebration of his recovery too.'

There'd been no way she could refuse that and so

she'd dredged up her bright beam and said, 'In that case, I'd love to.'

It went without saying that Ethan would be there. For one thing he and Cassandra worked together extremely well and for another, she thought wryly as she recalled the number of times he'd put her down, there was no show without Punch!

On the night in question, determined to throw off her depression, Gaby took endless pains with her appearance, and the end result was startling.

She'd braided the rich dark gloss of her hair on top of her head and, in a tight, flame-red dress, low-cut, with narrow straps over the shoulders, she looked sophisticated and much older.

As she pulled the sheerest of stockings onto her long legs and fastened them to a tiny, lacy suspender belt her hands became still. What *did* she look like? Had she gone too far in her efforts to impress Ethan? Because that was what it was all about.

Everything she did was aimed at him, and all for nothing. He seemed to get a perverse pleasure in putting her in her place and maybe it was time she gave up on him and found herself a callow, lusty youth, who wouldn't be everlastingly treating her like an infant.

Should she change into something less startling? Something more suitable for the kind of girl she was? No! He wasn't impressed with the person she was so why not see what he made of the person she wasn't? That was, of course, providing he noticed that she was there.

He noticed. . .with a look that brought bushy golden brows together in a straight line and the mouth that she yearned to kiss into a tight slit.

As she strolled into the bar of the hotel with a sort

of slinking grace that would have put Garbo in the shade, Ethan was with a group at the far end. It consisted of black-haired Lucinda...as expected... Cassandra and Bevan, the Bairds minus their offspring and the chairman of the Trust, a person of such loftiness that the nearest the likes of her had ever got to him was his photograph in the main hall of the hospital.

However, the prestigious company didn't stop Ethan from excusing himself and making a beeline for her the moment he saw her, and her first reaction was pleasure at his prompt acknowledgement of her arrival. The second was pique as he said tightly, 'Why are you dressed like that? You look as if you've come from the kind of place that you likened the inside of my house to.'

'Thanks a bunch,' she said calmly. 'There's no pleasing some people. You complain if I look or act in a youthful manner and yet you're still not satisfied when I put on the mantle of maturity.'

'Maturity!' he snarled through tight lips. 'You look like a moll...and tonight of all nights.'

Gaby eyed him innocently. 'My dad says that men who talk without moving their lips have usually been in prison.'

'Is that so?'

His eyes were glinting and she didn't think it was with amusement, but the urge to provoke was strong. She'd sallied forth tonight at peace with the world... well, almost. Certainly not with the devil at her elbow, but now she wanted to get under his skin and bring him in from the sidelines of her life.

'If you don't approve of my appearance I suggest you get back to your friends,' she told him sweetly. 'It won't do your image any good to be seen with a moll.'

Ethan's mouth hardened. 'Were we anywhere else but in this place I would be tempted to show you a side of my *image* that you haven't seen before,' he threatened, 'and I could still be driven to do so, élite company or not.'

Lucinda was trying to catch his eye at the other end of the bar and Gaby said, 'I think your presence is required by one of those same élite, so I'm going to leave you in peace while I have a wander round to see if anyone finds me more appetising than you do.'

She wanted to get away from him now, aware that misery was about to replace the cat-and-mouse exchange of words they'd been having. The night had started off on the wrong foot and was showing no signs of improving.

'Do so by all means,' he said flatly and, as he turned to go, added, 'I trust that you'll find the seating arrangements satisfactory when we go in for supper.'

That was enough to send her to where tables had been set for a meal later in the evening and when Gaby found her place she was incensed to discover that she'd been put next to the paramedic who had kissed her under the mistletoe.

It *had* to be Ethan's doing and, angry at the insinuation, she fought back by removing the card that bore his name from its place next to Lucinda and putting it next to her own, giving the orthopaedic consultant the pleasure of the other man's company instead.

The highlight of the evening was the moment when Ethan went to take his place and found it occupied by the paramedic. With a murmured apology to Lucinda, he seated himself into the vacant slot beside Gaby and said in a low voice, 'You really are asking for trouble. I don't know what's got into you. Have you been drinking?'

'No, I haven't!' she muttered indignantly.

'So, that being the case, let me buy you a drink. Your choice is stout, isn't it?'

Gaby stared at him.

'That is what you were drinking that first night in the Goose, if my memory serves me right,' and he beckoned to the waiter. 'A pint of stout for the young lady, please,' he said calmly.

She averted her eyes. She'd told him in teasing bravado that night that she was on pork scratchings and stout, rather than her usual orange juice, and now the fib was coming home to roost.

'Drink up,' he said blandly when the huge glass was placed in front of her and, as Gaby eyed the black liquid with its brown frothy top in dismay, 'No doubt a pint of stout is a mere appetiser to a woman of the world like yourself.'

'Absolutely,' she said calmly, trying not to shudder, 'and it will do my anaemia a power of good too,' and lifting the glass to her lips she drank half of its contents without stopping.

When she'd finished, Gaby wiped the froth off her lips with the back of her hand with feigned relish and wished herself miles away but Ethan was watching her and, with one of her best performances yet, she gave an appreciative burp and exclaimed fervently, 'Nectar!'

'There's plenty more where that came from,' he assured her with smooth generosity and she felt her stomach churn.

'Perhaps when I've eaten,' she said faintly.

He replied with impeccable politeness, 'of course. Just let me know when your glass is empty.'

As their eyes met she gave in. 'All right, you win,'

she told him. 'I was just kidding that night in the Goose. I prefer orange juice.'

Laughter rumbled low in his throat. 'What's the phrase? O what a tangled web? Or is it hoist with one's own petard?'

Gaby was ready to attack again. 'Why did you have me seated next to the paramedic?'

'I thought you and he seemed to be very chummy.'

'Because he caught me under the mistletoe? You have some nerve, Ethan! *You* don't fancy me but you don't like it if somebody else does, and in any case that day on the ward it was just a bit of fun for the benefit of the old folk.'

Their earlier sparring forgotten, he was serious now, his dark blue gaze holding her own as he said, 'You know damn well the effect you have on me but everytime I'm prepared to do something about it I'm sidetracked, which makes me think that maybe I'm not meant to.'

'There is nothing to "sidetrack" you tonight,' she told him softly, 'unless it's Lucinda or the hierarchy of the hospital.'

He gave a dry chuckle. 'I'll bear that in mind,' and as a waitress with a laden plate appeared at his elbow, 'and now, let's eat.'

As the night wore on Gaby had plenty of partners but never the one she wanted. It seemed to her that Ethan had danced with everyone except herself, but when they announced the last waltz he appeared at her elbow.

'I think this is ours,' he said gravely, and as he led her on to the dance floor and took her into his arms it seemed strange that after rocking and rolling most of the night away with other people they should be together for a sedate waltz.

Yet the music was right for her mood, soft and dreamy, and as Gaby gave herself up to the delight of being in his arms their earlier skirmishes were as if they'd never been.

Lucinda's cool dark eyes were on them as she went past in the arms of the chairman, and a couple of smartly dressed women out of Personnel were observing them curiously, but she didn't care. Wasn't it always the one with whom a man had the last waltz that he took home?

But they weren't going straight home, were they? They were going on to the gathering at the Marslands', and she wished they weren't.

Gaby longed for some time alone with him, and when they'd talked earlier it had seemed that he might feel the same, but her hopes of that were dashed when he said casually, 'I'm going to have a car-full when we go to Cassandra's place. There'll be yourself, needless to say, Lucinda, who came in a taxi and to whom I've offered a lift, and the Bairds, who aren't driving tonight so that they can have a drink.'

Her spirits plummeted. It was almost as if he'd contrived it so that they wouldn't be alone, but Ethan wasn't like that. He didn't beat about the bush and if he hadn't wanted to be with her he'd have said so... wouldn't he?

The small cottage that Cassandra and Bevan were hoping to leave soon for a bigger house was full by the time they got there and, because most of the people were from Springfield, Gaby soon felt at home.

She liked Mark and sensed that, from having seen her a few times at the hospital, the good-looking, dark-haired boy had a crush on her.

Adolescent love not being too far back in her life to remember, Gaby was especially nice to him and when they found themselves alone in the kitchen he asked her awkwardly if she would be his partner in the games that had been arranged.

'Sure,' she agreed easily. 'What are they going to be?'

'Charades, Trivial Pursuit. . .and things like that.'

She gave him her glowing smile. 'Together we will wipe the board!' she declared dramatically and when he started to laugh she joined in, thinking that no doubt when Ethan saw her with the boy he would conclude that she'd found her own level.

It had been snowing all the time they'd been at the cottage and when they came out in the early hours of the morning the sleeping village lay beneath a cold white carpet.

'Damn!' Lucinda said when she saw it. 'The flats where I live are on a steep road. If they don't get the gritters out before morning I won't be able to get to the infirmary.'

Jean Baird and her husband weren't too pleased either as the road to their house soon became impassable in winter-time. Only Gaby felt delight. In one week's time it would be Christmas Day and what more traditional setting for it than snow-covered streets and roofs, with the white-tipped Cotswolds dominating the skyline?

She was waiting to see in what order Ethan would drop off his passengers, knowing that if she was first the evening would be ruined, but he took the Bairds to their place first and skirting Cleeve House, dropped Lucinda off outside the upmarket flat that she'd referred to and at last they were alone.

But to Gaby's chagrin she couldn't keep her eyes open, and when Ethan pulled up outside her lodgings she was curled up beside him fast asleep, the tight red dress riding up to show her long legs and its neckline revealing the drooping white column of her throat.

When she felt his lips brush against her cheek her eyes flew open and she groaned, 'How could I fall asleep? You must think me absolutely useless.'

'Never that,' he said gravely as he looked down on her. 'I saw how you took the trouble to make Mark's night a success. Lots of girls would have patronised him, but not you.'

'You noticed?'

'I notice everything about you and, believe me, it does nothing for my peace of mind.'

Gaby was wide awake now. She'd been desperate to be alone with him and she'd got her wish...and she wasn't going to waste the opportunity.

'Tell me about it,' she breathed.

'Words aren't necessary,' he said huskily. 'This is all you need to know.' And, cupping her face in his hands, he bent his head and kissed her, possessing her lips the way he possessed her mind, her dreams and her future—if he would only remove the blinkers.

'I want to spend Christmas with you,' he whispered as his lips moved to her throat and his hands cupped her breasts.

'Just Christmas?' she asked dreamily.

He laughed, the laugh of the conquering male, and yet there was tenderness in it and the joy of belonging. 'For starters, yes.'

'I'll have to go,' he said after they'd kissed again with rising passion, 'or your landlady will be coming out to see what's going on.' As she nodded reluctantly he said, 'Sleep well, Gaby, for what's left of the night. I'll see you in the morning.'

As she snuggled beneath the quilt Gaby hugged the words to herself. 'I'll see you in the morning,' he'd said. They had a magical sound. That was what she'd dreamed of, their seeing each other in the morning, the afternoon, the evening, the night...always and for ever...and it was going to happen. She could feel it in her bones because hadn't Ethan said that he wanted to spend Christmas with her? And that would be only the beginning.

What could she buy him? What gift was there that would tell him how much she cared? Tomorrow she would go Christmas shopping. She'd had no interest in doing so before but now she wanted to buy up the town and, as the snowflakes continued to swirl past her window she slept.

Gaby awoke to the delicious thought that she and Ethan were going to spend Christmas together. It was all coming right at the most magical time of the year. She couldn't wait to see him again and as she showered and put on her uniform her head was full of plans... where they would go...what they would do...what she would wear.

When she went downstairs she found Sally in a flap, and smartly dressed for the hour of the day. On seeing her one remaining boarder, she said breathlessly, 'You'll never guess what, Gaby. My scatterbrained young sister rang at half-past six this morning to say that she's getting married this afternoon at the registry office!

'Can you believe it? Doesn't let me know until the day of the event and she knows darned well I'd be heartbroken if I wasn't there. Robert is on the phone now trying to arrange a few days off work so that we can stay up there over Christmas.'

'Where is "up there"?' Gaby asked.

'Sheffield. We're going to have to leave in a matter

of minutes. Will you be all right here on your own over Christmas?' she asked anxiously.

Gaby smiled. She would be more than all right. The odds were she would be spending a minimum amount of time in Cleeve House with Ethan's delightful residence available to them and, having no wish to add to Sally's problems, she told her, 'Of course I will. Just get off to the wedding. You've a long journey ahead of you.'

Sally gave her a quick hug. 'Some landlady I'm turning out to be, aren't I? Leaving my favourite boarder to fend for herself at a time like this? But you do understand, don't you? I must be there for my sister, although she's going to get a piece of my mind for not letting me know sooner.'

At that moment Robert appeared to confirm that he'd arranged some leave and as they both grabbed their top coats and the case that Sally must have packed at some unearthly hour she said, 'There's egg and bacon in the oven, Gaby, and help yourself to anything else you fancy. We'll be back the day after Boxing Day.'

There was a pile of Christmas mail on the mat in the hall and Sally bent and picked it up quickly, thrusting it into the tavelling bag that she was carrying.

'As we're going to be away all over Christmas I've packed our presents, the Christmas cake, and a plum pudding,' she said, 'so we might as well take some cards to go with them.'

As Gaby walked to the hospital the snow was crisp and firm beneath her feet, with a winter sun glinting on its whiteness. Gary, the younger of the two porters, was larking about at the gates and within minutes Gaby and he were snowballing, laughing and hooting as they chased each other.

For once Ethan wasn't around to observe her youthful high spirits and this time she wished he was because she knew now that his criticisms of her were his way of concealing his feelings.

The mere thought of him made her realise how desperate she was to see him again and she dropped the handful of snow she'd just picked up and, pointing to the clock in the entrance hall for Gary's benefit, she went inside.

Ethan wasn't in his office but that wasn't unusual. It often happened that the moment he set foot in the place his presence was required somewhere by someone.

She could wait. This was her last day. Tonight she would be finishing until the day after Boxing Day, and she knew that he was off for a similar period as they were both down for working over New Year.

Carol singers from the village church arrived in the middle of the morning and the nurses joined them in entertaining the patients in both wards. James Harrison, the hypothermia patient, was much better and, with the strain of making ends meet taken away for a few days, was enjoying himself hugely in the festive surroundings. When the age-old words and music filled the air he surprised them all by joining in with an excellent baritone voice which was a delight to the ear.

Gaby was happier than she'd been in a long time. The memory of the long, sad months in Sorrento and her father's infrequent communication with her didn't hurt so much now because she had Ethan. It was Christmas and she wasn't going to be alone. She was going to be with the man she loved, and what more romantic season than this was there for him to tell her that he returned her feelings?

After the carol-singing Cassandra had arranged for coffee and hot mince pies to be served to patients and visitors alike, and as there were no seriously ill cases at that precise moment the atmosphere was friendly and relaxed.

Gaby had expected Ethan to appear while the singing had been taking place and every time anyone came into the wards her eyes flicked across, but so far he hadn't arrived and she wondered what was keeping him.

'I had a super time last night at your place, Cassandra,' she said when they managed to get a moment alone. 'Mark is a lovely lad. He was telling me that he wants to be a doctor, like Bevan.'

Cassandra laughed. 'Yes, he does, but if he had the chance to be a professional rugby player instead I've a good idea which he would choose but, seriously, I would love him to take up medicine in some form or other.'

Gaby was bursting to tell somebody her good news and who better than Cassandra, who was already aware of her feelings for Ethan? And so she said with a happy beam, 'Guess what? Ethan and I are going to spend Christmas together. Isn't it fabulous?'

The sister-in-charge was eyeing her uncomfortably and Gaby asked, 'Aren't you glad for me?'

'Yes, of course I am,' she said with a lukewarm sort of ethusiasm and then, without meeting her eyes, 'It's just that he's gone away and, according to the message I found waiting for me when I came in this morning, he won't be back until after Christmas. Had he not told you?'

Gaby felt the blood drain from her face and then it

flooded back in an embarrassing, shaming tide. 'No, he hadn't mentioned it,' she said, making no pretence with regard to her discomfiture. Treacherous tears were threatening to spill and she took a deep breath. 'He only suggested it last night and yet he must have known that he wasn't going to be around!'

'It doesn't sound like Ethan to do that,' Cassandra said loyally. 'I'm sure there must be a very good reason for it.'

'Yes, there is,' Gaby told her with flat bitterness. 'From the day we met he has never treated me any other way than as a child but in my book children, of all people, should be able to trust those they love. Would you happen to know where he's gone?'

'Kashmir, I believe.'

Gaby stared at her. 'Kashmir? Why would he go there, of all places?'

Cassandra's discomfiture was becoming more obvious by the minute. 'I don't know, Gaby, but I think I should tell you that he hasn't gone alone.'

If a hole had opened beneath her feet and swallowed her up Gaby would have been glad. This was the final humiliation, as Cassandra's manner told her that it had to be a woman.

'Who has he gone with?' she whispered raggedly with the last shreds of her dignity.

'Lucinda,' the other woman told her reluctantly and then, as if she thought that the devastated young nurse in front of her wasn't capable of taking it in, she repeated, 'Lucinda Beckman.'

Gaby was reeling. Lucinda! Ethan had decided to spend Christmas with the brash orthopaedic consultant. Well, there was one thing, she thought dazedly, he'd got a woman of the world there! He wouldn't ever be able to liken Lucinda to an infantile bit of a kid.

CHAPTER TEN

IT WAS the longest day of Gaby's life. She couldn't wait to get back to the solitude of Cleeve House to lick her wounds. When they'd met in the restaurant at lunch time Cassandra had suggested with thoughtful sincerity, 'Why don't you spend Christmas with us, Gaby? Bevan and I would love to have you and it goes without saying that Mark would approve of the idea as I think you are the subject of his first youthful passion.'

She had managed a smile but it had been an effort. 'Thanks, but no,' she'd said. 'I wouldn't want to intrude into your family's festivities, and...' She'd swallowed and then gallantly continued, 'Now that I know where I stand with Ethan I'll follow up other plans that I'd made previously.'

'Are you sure?' Cassandra had asked anxiously.

'Yes, I'm positive,' she'd said, with the sure knowledge that if she'd tried to eat the food in front of her she would have choked.

Gaby felt that she'd put on a reasonable enough show for Cassandra but was aware that one or two of the staff were eyeing her curiously, and she supposed it wasn't surprising as everyone must have seen her in Ethan's company of recent weeks. Therefore the news that he'd gone to far-away Kashmir to spend Christmas with Lucinda Beckman must be more than a little surprising.

In spite of her aching disillusionment, all the day wasn't gloom. Gaby's generous heart rejoiced with everyone else's when the news came through that Joan Jarvis had given birth to a son.

'They induced her at half-nine this morning,' Cassandra said joyfully, 'and she had a boy half an hour ago. They're going to call him Noel for obvious reasons.'

'Are they both all right?' Gaby asked.

'Yes, thank God! Joan was at thirty-seven weeks so the baby isn't as premature as it might have been.'

'And now, hopefully, the pre-eclampsia will disappear.'

'Yes, indeed.'

Gaby turned away to hide tears. Whatever *she* might have to be miserable about it was good to know that Joan and her husband had been given the greatest gift of all time for *their* Christmas. Nothing was more wonderful than the birth of a child, and her thoughts went to the unfortunate Erica who would have been unable to give Ethan the children he craved.

If this thing with Lucinda wasn't just a one-off, it was to be hoped that *she* could produce children. Though, knowing her, it was possible that the ambitious doctor wouldn't want them if she could.

The memory of his past ruthlessness brought back to mind his more recent display of it with regard to herself, and as her last working day before Christmas showed signs of drawing to a lacklustre end Gaby decided what she was going to do with the five empty days that lay ahead, and it had nothing to do with going to stay in the utilitarian living accommodation above her father's shop.

In any case she hadn't been invited, and even if she had the thought of its ever-present steaminess would have made her think twice. No, she was going to go to the place where she'd been happiest. The idea might be a travesty, compared to what she'd been expecting of the yule-tide before Ethan had let her down or a self-inflicted torture in her present state of melancholy, but that was what she was going to do.

There was just half an hour to go when the day's lack of medical trauma changed. They'd all been thinking that it was too good to be true, and at half-past four in the afternoon the toll of the slippery pavements and frozen slopes outside was brought to their notice.

The first patients to arrive in Casualty were two young boys who'd been sledging on the hillside behind Springfield. They'd been using a makeshift affair without any proper steering and had hit a tree. One of them was unconscious and the other had what looked like a broken leg.

Bevan Marsland was the GP present when they were brought in and he immediately arranged for the boy with the suspected fracture to be taken to the infirmary. 'Lucinda won't be there,' Cassandra pointed out in a low voice. 'She's gone gallivanting off to Kashmir with Ethan.'

Gaby heard the comment and she flinched but Bevan, in the process of examining the more seriously injured of the two boys, pointed out to his wife that Lucinda wasn't the only doctor on the orthopaedic unit at the infirmary.

'We're going to need a skull X-ray here,' he said as the lad began to moan painfully. 'If it shows a closed fracture the necessity for a CT scan shouldn't arise but, alternatively, if there is an open fracture then it will be over to the neurology boys. So let's keep our fingers crossed for him, shall we?' he said.

His face was grim and Gaby guessed that his mind was going back to Mark's accident, to the horror of it, and its subsequent fortunate conclusion.

'And if he *does* need a CT scan?' Gaby asked.

'It will be the same as when Mark was injured,' he explained. 'We'll have to move him to the infirmary and hand him over to Nicholas Page and his team.'

In the next quarter of an hour there was another case of hypothermia, similar to that of James Harrison, and then came a woman driver with a whiplash injury to the neck sustained when the car behind had shunted into her vehicle on the icy road.

All in all, they were reminders that though it was cosy and organised inside Springfield there was chaos outside on the icy roads and pavements due to the weather conditions and as the snow had started to fall again it could only get worse.

The glistening white carpet had melted during the day and now there was new snow upon rapidly freezing slush. As Gaby trudged back to Cleeve House its earlier enchantment had gone. It seemed a lifetime since she and Gary had been frolicking at the hospital gates.

She'd been happy then. The blow hadn't fallen and since it had she hadn't been able to work up any interest in anything except the safe arrival of the Jarvis baby and the sick and injured she'd left behind at Springfield.

The X-ray had shown that the boy who'd received the blow to the head had a closed fracture of the skull and, although suffering from concussion, in a few days' time he would be able to go home to celebrate the Christmas that he'd almost missed.

His friend would be hobbling around on crutches with his leg in plaster, and the woman motorist would be wearing a surgical collar over the Christmas break instead of her favourite necklace.

It had turned out that the second hypothermia victim

was the one who had given most cause for concern. She was an elderly lady from a cottage just down the road and was in a much more serious condition than James Harrison had been.

Poor living conditions and hypothyroidism, which could cause rapid deterioration in the body's heating function, had caused the problem, and within seconds of her being brought into Springfield her heart had stopped beating.

Artificial respiration had been started immediately by Michael Drew and another GP, but to no avail. The lady's general frailty, along with prolonged exposure to the cold and some degree of malnutrition, had taken their toll, and when Michael had reluctantly pronounced life extinct the Christmas spirit, which had been so much in evidence amongst staff and patients, was replaced by dismay and consternation.

As Gaby let herself into the empty house it seemed eerie without Sally bustling about and appetising smells coming from the kitchen, but that didn't matter as she wasn't hungry. She hadn't eaten since breakfast and until she'd sorted out her arrangements there wouldn't be time.

When she finally went to bed after forcing down a slice of toast and a cup of Oxo, there was a bleak sort of satisfaction inside her. At least she'd done something positive. She wasn't going to be sitting around an empty house all over Christmas moping over Ethan. She was going to pick up the pieces and be damned if she was ever going to let herself get in this state again over any man.

The promise she'd made herself lasted until she stood looking out over the Bay of Naples from the window of a small apartment which she'd rented for the Christmas period.

It was then that it disintegrated beneath a great surge of loneliness as she looked out to where Capri nestled in the distance and the pyramid-like shape of Vesuvius rose out of a winter mist across the bay.

Sorrento was a place that she'd always associated with happiness until recently, but, with her *nonna's* death and now her return to it in such a low frame of mind, Gaby was already thinking that coming here was a mistake.

Though what had she expected? That its magic would work for her like it always had? Even Ethan wouldn't expect her to be that gauche.

'Life is what you make it,' she told herself resolutely as she grabbed a jacket and went out on to the balcony, 'and if you're going to sit and mope all over Christmas you might as well have stayed back in England.'

As she walked along the bustling main street the sun was warm on her back in spite of the time of year and Gaby told herself that at least she wouldn't be frozen in her misery out here. It was a milder climate and she needed something to take the chill out of her heart.

A big silver Fiat screeched to a halt ahead of her and when its driver leapt out and came towards her Gaby's eyes widened. It was Giorgio, looking vulgarly prosperous and as confident as ever.

'Gabriella!' he enthused. 'How long have you been back in Sorrento?'

'Three hours, twenty-five minutes and two seconds,' she told him laconically, 'and, before you start jumping to conclusions, Giorgio, I'm not here to see *you*.'

His handsome face fell. 'Then who are you here to see?'

'Nobody.'

'You are alone?'

'Yes.'

'Then you must dine at the hotel tonight,' he insisted. 'We live in a villa nearby. I will introduce you to my wife.'

'Thanks just the same,' she told him flatly, 'but I don't think so. I'm here for a rest.'

He goggled at her. 'A rest! You speak like the old lady!'

'Maybe I do. I've aged a lot recently.'

'You are crazy!' he said snappishly. 'We could take up where we left off.'

'And you are arrogant,' she snapped back angrily. 'You made your bed when you married your wealthy wife...and you can lie on it. One thing is for sure— you're not going to get near mine.' And she walked on, leaving him fuming on the pavement.

God! Giorgio was something else! A handsome lecher who thought that every woman he met couldn't resist him. They hadn't seen each other in months but that hadn't deterred him from propositioning her.

Yet Ethan wasn't exactly behind the door when it came to women, was he? What with his spurned fiancée, Gaby herself drooling over him like the village idiot and now Clever Clogs Lucinda. There was no telling who he was going to captivate next.

As the pale sun shrank on the horizon and darkness fell Gaby went back to the apartment to phone Cassandra. She hadn't told her where she planned to go, but now that she'd arrived in Italy it seemed only fair to inform her, in case she and her family went round to Cleeve House over Christmas and found her gone.

'You're in Italy!' she cried in astonishment when

Gaby explained where she was. 'You never said *that* was what you were planning!'

'I only decided to come here after I left work yesterday,' Gaby said quietly. 'I rang Gatwick and got a cancellation flight, and when I got here I booked into an apartment in a small complex above the harbour. After what you'd told me about Ethan there was nothing to keep me in England, but I did feel that you should know where I was in case you were concerned about my absence.'

'I most certainly would have been if I'd gone round there and found you missing,' Cassandra said, 'especially after your leaving Springfield in such low spirits.'

'Yes, well, I'm fine now,' she lied, 'so don't worry about me, Cassandra.'

'Are you sure?' she insisted.

'Yes, I'm sure.'

'All right, but give me your address, will you? I'll feel better if I've got some sort of contact with you... and Gaby...'

'Yes?'

'If you want to talk I'm here, just a phone call away.'

'Thanks,' she choked, 'but if there is one thing I don't want to do it's burden you with my problems, especially at Christmas.'

'Nevertheless the offer still stands,' the other woman told her firmly and, as Gaby bade her goodbye, the ice around her heart didn't seem quite so cold.

She went to bed early with the depressing knowledge inside her that tomorrow was Christmas Eve. There would be parties and celebrations taking place all along the Bay of Naples, and unless she threw off her misery she would be alone and like a fish out of water.

It was typical of Lucinda to want to spend Christmas

in some far-away place like Kashmir, Gaby thought as sleep evaded her. That sort of thing went with her image. She couldn't see her settling for Blackpool or Weston Super Mare for a romantic interlude.

You should have introduced her to Giorgio, she told herself. They would make a good pair...two lusting egomaniacs together! But, whatever Lucinda was, Gaby had to remind herself that she'd been Ethan's choice. *She* was the one he'd decided to spend Christmas with and there was no way of getting away from that fact.

The next morning she went to walk down by the harbour from where the hydrofoils sailed to Capri. It was noisy and colourful and, after the silence of the small apartment, oddly comforting.

After eating in a bar in a tree-lined courtyard she went to visit her *nonna's* grave, and, as the winter sun glinted on all the fine marbles around her, Gaby placed a posy of flowers in a vase on the wall beside which the grave stood in its own small alcove.

In the tradition of the country there was a photograph of the old lady there, and there was a huge lump in Gaby's throat as she gazed on the smiling, lined face beneath a coronet of thick grey braids.

This was real, she thought tearfully. Here lay someone that she'd always been able to rely on. Her *nonna* had never let her down. She'd always been there for her...unlike some she could mention.

It saddened her to know that her mother wasn't there with her but in a bleak churchyard in Birmingham. She'd vowed times without number that one day she would bring her body back to the beautiful land from which she'd come. Only her father could have been so insensitive as to have denied her mother and her *nonna* that.

She had decided that she wasn't going to sit in and mope, not on Christmas Eve, but how to put that decision into practice she wasn't sure. The hotels would be full of revellers but the odds were they would all have made reservations or bought tickets for food, wine and entertainment and, in any case, did she want to be amongst a happy crowd?

Not particularly, but she got dressed for a festive evening, nevertheless, in a dress of pale blue silk with silver jewellery and matching shoes.

There was nothing vibrant about its colour; it was pale and subdued, giving her an ethereal look, and her pallor added to the effect so that when she sallied forth on foot for she knew not where Gaby felt that she was at one with the grey mist that hung over the bay.

It was an eerie sort of night, and the street café across the way seemed a place of shifting shadows. There was a man sitting at one of the tables, a big man, and when the mist around him lifted for a moment Gaby saw the gleam of gold upon his head.

Her step faltered, and she chided herself for letting the sight of a fair-haired man amongst the dark Neapolitans throw her into confusion. But he was getting to his feet and as she watched, transfixed, he began to move towards her.

'Gabriella!' he said in a low voice, and her heart jolted in her breast. Then it was leaping like a wild thing, but she had no words. For once in her life she was completely speechless and as he came across and took her hands firmly into his, her eyes were huge in the lights of the tree-lined road.

'I've been travelling for three days non-stop,' he

was telling her, 'and all the time dreading that I wouldn't get to you in time to keep my promise.'

Gaby found her voice at last. 'But Cassandra said you'd gone to Kashmir with Lucinda.'

He frowned. 'Cassandra said...? I left her a brief note, yes, but surely you didn't need to consult *her*? I explained what had happened in my letter to you. I put it through the letter-box at Cleeve House in the early hours of the morning. Not long after I'd left you, in fact.'

'I didn't receive any letter,' she said woodenly, as a sudden vision of Sally scooping the mail up off the mat and stuffing it into her bag without looking came to mind.

His face was grey with fatigue, but it went even paler as he said, 'So you don't know what happened? Why I left like I did?'

'No, I don't,' she informed him in the same stilted manner. 'Are you going to tell me?'

He groaned. 'Am I? Of course I am! I'm appalled to think how low your opinion of me must be.'

She was rallying. 'Well, let's say that it's had a bit of a battering, but I'm willing to listen.'

He took her to a seat in a small olive grove overlooking the sea, and it took Gaby all her time not to enfold him in her arms and assure him that it didn't matter. Nothing mattered now that he was here. But things had to be clear between them, honest and straightforward, or there would be no foundations to their love.

With his arm protectively around her shoulders, he began, 'After I got home from the party at Cassandra's place, I'd barely had time to put my head on the pillow when Lucinda was on the phone in a terrible state. She'd just had a phone call from government sources to say that her young brother, who is all she has in the world, had been captured by terrorists in Kashmir.

'Apparently he's on one of these back-packing-round-the-world trips, and he and another guy had strayed into an area where they shouldn't. She was frantic, and ready to set off there at that very moment.

'She begged me to go with her for moral support, and what could I do? My mind was full of you and me, our future together. I'd finally given in to my total need of you and was going to forget past hurts and the difference in our ages and let the enchantment of being with you for the rest of my life take over.

'But I couldn't refuse. The situation she found herself in was the kind of thing that nightmares are made of and she'd no one else to turn to. So, while she was booking flights to Islamabad—which is about the nearest one can fly to where he was—I scribbled a quick letter to you, asking you to understand and promising to get back the first chance I had.

'It was a promise I kept and, low and behold, when I got back to Gloucestershire it was *your* turn to be missing. Thank God you'd told Cassie where you were staying, otherwise I would have been searching Sorrento.

'I was sitting out there getting my breath back and waiting for you to come out and there you were, like a beautiful silver ghost watching me.'

'What would you have done if I hadn't appeared?' she asked softly.

'I intended giving you a couple of seconds to show your face and then I would have gone in to find you. I've been away from you long enough.'

'And what happened about Lucinda's brother?' she asked, dragging her mind back to the reason for his absence.

'It was good news when we got there. The authorities at Islamabad told us that there'd been some kind of mix-up and he'd been released. I left Lucinda waiting to be reunited with him and caught the first flight back, and I'd no sooner got home than I was dashing back to Gatwick to get a flight for Italy.'

Gaby snuggled against him. 'I've never been so miserable in my whole life. I thought that you were using me, that you thought I was somebody you could pick up and put down when you felt like it because you knew I was crazy about you.'

He shook his head. 'I would never treat anyone like that, least of all you, but before I tell you how much you mean to me there is something that you need to know,' he said gravely.

She moved out of the circle of his arm and eyed him warily. 'You're going to ask me to prove that I can have children?'

'No. I'm not!' he said in angry protest. 'What kind of man do you think I am? An overbearing one who demands perfection from those he loves?

'What I want you to know is this... Yes, I did call off my marriage to Erica because she couldn't have children, but there was a very good reason.'

'And what is it?' Gaby asked quietly.

'You've seen how frail she is, haven't you?' he said soberly. 'Well, I was to find out that she wasn't as fragile as all that.

'Whenever I tried to discuss our future and my great desire for a family she always veered away from the subject, and, fool that I was, I made allowances for it because I thought that she was apprehensive for her health with regard to having children.

'However, the weekend before the wedding we went out for a meal with a group of friends and she was the life and soul of the party. Watching her laughing and posing, one of the guys said jokingly, "Are you sure that you're all geared up for domesticity, Erica? Somehow I can't imagine you pushing a pram."

'"I won't be," she flashed back immediately, and when her eyes met mine she looked away.

'I realised afterwards that the wine she'd been partaking of freely must have made her drop her guard, and when we were on the way home I tackled her about what she'd said.

'It all came out then and I was stunned. She'd been sterilised some time before we met and, where naturally I was prepared to accept that it must have been for medical reasons, she told me defiantly that it wasn't that at all. She wanted an unrestricted sex life...and no children.

'I could maybe have forgiven her for that as she had the right to decide what she did with her own body, but to string me along with my high hopes of family life when she knew it could never be was something I wasn't going to accept on any terms. That is why we parted company.'

Gaby's eyes were dark with outrage. 'How could any woman do that to the man she loved?' she cried.

His smile was rueful. 'I doubt that she loved me. Erica was attracted to me, very much so, but I must have been a huge disappointment all round, refusing to sleep with her before the wedding because I respected what I saw as her frailty and bleating on about how much I wanted children all the time.

'She did me a favour, though, in the long run. The way I felt about her was nothing compared to the way

I feel about you, Gabriella,' he said gently as he nuzzled her soft neck with his lips. 'You are fever in my blood, joy in my heart, peace to my soul. I feel as if I've waited all my life for you.'

Gaby twisted round to face him. Her mind was awash with delight, and as she ran her fingers over the serious lines of his face she said wonderingly, 'And to think I judged you as the original male chauvinist. I thought that you were so high and mighty that only the best and perfect was good enough for you and that you were holding some physical fault against a hapless woman.'

He was smiling now and in the light of the streetlamps there was the look in his eyes that she'd longed to see. 'I do want the best and perfect,' he teased softly, 'and you are it, my sweet, young love.

'You've brought joy and laughter into my life, passion and excitement, and I don't care a damn whether you can give me children or not. It's you that I want, my beautiful girl, and if children come from our union that will be marvellous, but I'm prepared to let that sort of thing take its normal course.

'You *are* going to marry me, aren't you, Gabriella?' he asked as his arms tightened around her.

His hands slid beneath her shoulders and he cradled her to him as she murmured, 'Just try and stop me, Ethan.'

'I've wanted you ever since that first day in the churchyard,' he told her as they walked along the deserted seafront some time later. 'I'd been watching the wedding of Cassandra and Bevan, thinking how I envied them their deep love for each other and the strong physical attraction between them, and when I turned round *you* were there, standing beside me, as if the Fates had read my mind and generously granted my wish.'

'I thought you were a jilted suitor,' she told him laughingly. 'Some guy who was in love with the bride and had been spurned, and I immediately wanted to make you happy again—make you laugh, unwind. When I saw you in the Goose the same evening I had to speak to you again, had to bring myself to your notice. It was as if somebody was pulling my strings—' her eyes softened '—and they've been pulling them ever since.'

She stopped and, putting her arms around his neck, she said with a catch in her voice, 'Whither *thou* goest, *I* want to go, Ethan. Whatsoever *thou* doest, *I* want to do.'

'And that is how it's going to be,' he promised tenderly. 'How soon can we be married? Can we arrange for it to take place here in Sorrento? Our Christmas present to ourselves?'

'We can try,' she said as the mist lifted from over the Bay of Naples and a sky full of stars twinkled above them, 'and if it isn't possible we've got all the rest of our lives to arrange it.

'Don't the words have a lovely sound, Ethan?' she whispered as he adored her with his eyes. 'We've got all the rest of our lives.'

'Yes, they do,' he agreed, and then, with mock seriousness, 'Perhaps this is the moment when I should confess that I'm not just marrying you because I love you.'

Her head came round at that and there was a question in the dreamy, dark eyes. 'What other reasons could there be?'

'Well, first of all I'll be gaining an interior decorator,' he said, and, as she began to laugh, added, 'And secondly, I won't have to pay for my dry cleaning.'

'It's clear that you don't know my dad!' she hooted. 'He drives a hard bargain. It would be a case of a private ward in exchange for retexturing!'

GET 4 BOOKS AND A MYSTERY GIFT

Return this coupon and we'll send you 4 Medical Romance™ novels and a mystery gift absolutely FREE! We'll even pay the postage and packing for you.

We're making you this offer to introduce you to the benefits of Reader Service: FREE home delivery of brand-new Medical Romance novels, at least a month before they are available in the shops, FREE gifts and a monthly Newsletter packed with information.

Accepting these FREE books and gift places you under no obligation to buy, you may cancel at any time, even after receiving just your free shipment. Simply complete the coupon below and send it to:

MILLS & BOON® READER SERVICE, FREEPOST, CROYDON, SURREY, CR9 3WZ.

No stamp needed

Yes, please send me 4 free Medical Romance novels and a mystery gift. I understand that unless you hear from me, I will receive 4 superb new titles every month for just £2.10* each, postage and packing free. I am under no obligation to purchase any books and I may cancel or suspend my subscription at any time, but the free books and gift will be mine to keep in any case. (I am over 18 years of age)

M6LE

Ms/Mrs/Miss/Mr _____

Address _____

_____

_____ Postcode _____

Offer closes 30th June 1997. We reserve the right to refuse an application. *Prices and terms subject to change without notice. Offer only valid in UK and Ireland and is not available to current subscribers to this series. **Readers in Ireland please write to:** P.O. Box 4546, Dublin 24. Overseas readers please write for details.

You may be mailed with offers from other reputable companies as a result of this application. Please tick box if you would prefer not to receive such offers. ☐

MILLS & BOON

Medical Romance

Books for enjoyment this month...

RESPONDING TO TREATMENT	Abigail Gordon
BRIDAL REMEDY	Marion Lennox
A WISH FOR CHRISTMAS	Josie Metcalfe
WINGS OF DUTY	Meredith Webber

Treats in store!

Watch next month for these absorbing stories...

TAKE A CHANCE ON LOVE	Jean Evans
PARTNERS IN LOVE	Maggie Kingsley
DRASTIC MEASURES	Laura MacDonald
PERFECT PARTNERS	Carol Wood

Available from:
W.H. Smith, John Menzies, Volume One, Forbuoys, Martins,
Woolworths, Tesco, Asda, Safeway and other paperback stockists.

Readers in South Africa - write to:
IBS, Private Bag X3010, Randburg 2125.